BOUJEE WITH A LIL HOOD IN HER 3

Written By: Lady Lissa & Kia Meche

D1714809

It's easy to join our mailing list!

Just send your email address by text message:

Text

TMPBOOKS

to 22828 to get started.

Recap From Book Two

Fendi paced back and forth inside her house, wondering if Syd was okay. She also wondered if the cops would be showing up to her door to arrest her. She didn't mean to shoot him, but she was upset; really upset. She had asked him several times to leave and he wouldn't, so she was justified for shooting him. He was lucky that she shot him in the foot and nowhere else. The way she was feeling, she could have shot him in the damn heart for breaking hers the way that he did. She couldn't believe he had the nerve to take that bitch Hennessy out on a date.

"What the fuck was he thinking? Did he really think he could do some shit like that and get away with it?" she asked herself.

She wanted to call Syd and make sure he was alright, but changed her mind. "He deserved that shit! Fuck him and that dirty bitch!" she said out loud.

She began to giggle at the sight of Hennessy when she was done whipping her ass. She had really laid into that bitch. "That'll teach her to fuck with me or my man again," she said with a laugh.

But then, her laugh disappeared as she reevaluated that last statement. Syd wasn't even her man anymore. The two of them had broken up and she needed to just let it go. Fendi felt a little flushed, so she went into the kitchen, splashed some water on her face and grabbed a glass, filling it with ice and water from the dispenser on the fridge. She drank the water, but still felt a little weak. She sat down on the bar stool to drink her water.

With all the excitement she just had, she figured it was from that. Hopefully, the feeling would pass by morning and everything would be okay. However, when she stood up, she had to catch herself because she almost fainted and hit the floor. She decided the best thing for her to do was to go to bed. She changed into her boy shorts and tank top and hopped between the down comforter and her 1500 thread count Egyptian cotton sheets. She snuggled further into the bed and fell asleep.

****

Early the next morning, she woke up and called in at work. There was no way she was going to make it in today. Not only did her muscles hurt from fighting yesterday, but she was still a little weak. She wasn't sure what was going on, but decided to get up and soak in a hot bubble bath and if that didn't help, she'd go to the doctor. Maybe, she was coming down with the flu or something. She filled the tub with jasmine and vanilla scented bubbles and sat in it.

She relaxed her head against the bath pillow and closed her eyes. Thoughts of her and Syd during happier times replayed itself over and over in her mind. She couldn't believe that it was really over between them. A lone tear slipped from her eye, but she quickly brushed it away. She wasn't going to cry over that man anymore. The two of them had a good run, but it was time for them to both move on. She had never fired her gun in the two years that she had it.

It was actually Syd's idea that she get the gun for protection, since she was working at Club Lush. He wanted to make sure if something ever happened to her, she would be able to protect herself. She never realized the first person she would use it on would be the man she loved. How had things between them gotten so out of control? After soaking in the tub for about an hour and a half, she finally emerged. Her skin looked like a dried up prune, but she felt a little better.

She dried herself off, then applied body lotion to her moistened skin. She brushed her teeth, cleansed her face, then got dressed. After eating a bowl of Special K and a banana, she decided to go see Doctor Lancer. She would need an excuse for work anyway, so she decided to go find out what was going on with her body.

She didn't have an appointment, but she was a favorite of the doctor, so she knew she wouldn't have long to wait. She walked in and greeted Aimee, the receptionist.

"Hello Aimee," Fendi said as she signed her name on the log in sheet.

"You didn't make an appointment today, Miss Peters?" Aimee asked.

"No, I didn't have time. I just woke up feeling a little under the weather and figured I'd let Doctor Lancer squeeze me in," Fendi said with a fake smile.

She liked Aimee, but definitely was not trying to have any conversation this morning.

"Well, she actually had a cancellation this morning, so I'll just slip your name in the book and let her know that you're here," Aimee said.

"Thank you." She sat down and picked up the People's Magazine with the Obama's on the cover. She was so sad that President Obama was finished with his terms. She hated to see him and his family go, because she had gotten attached to them. Before she could begin flipping through the magazine, her name was being called to the back.

She put the magazine down on the table and walked to the back.

"Hello Miss Peters," Natasha greeted her. Natasha was Doctor Lancer's nurse and her sister in law. Fendi liked her because she was always so patient and friendly.

"Good morning, Natasha. How are you?"

"I'm good. What seems to be bothering you today?"

Fendi sat down in the chair as she began to tell Natasha how she had been feeling. "How long have you been feeling this way?"

"It actually started last night. I felt so weak, I almost passed out," Fendi explained.

"Well, let's check your blood pressure and temp. Then, I'll weigh you and have you give me a urine sample before I put you in a room," Natasha said.

"Ugh! Do I have to do a urine test? I hate pissing in that little cup," Fendi said.

"I'll give you a pair of gloves, as usual, so you won't touch a thing."

"Okay. I mean, if it's necessary for you to find out what's wrong with me."

"It is. We just need to make sure that you don't have any kind of infections or anything like that," Natasha explained.

Fendi finished up the triage part of the exam and placed the gloves on her hand. She took the urine cup Natasha had given her and placed it under her bottom as she stooped over the toilet. Once the cup was halfway filled with urine, she set it on the sink, wiped herself off, and then flushed the toilet. She placed the cap on the cup and sat it on the window of the lab. She knocked on the little wooden door, removed the gloves and washed her hands.

She exited the restroom and followed Natasha to the exam room. "Doctor Lancer will be with you shortly," Natasha said as she prepared to walk out. "Oh, Miss Peters, I forgot to ask. When was your last menstrual cycle?"

Fendi tried to think back to when was her last cycle, but she couldn't. "I'm sorry. My mind is a little fuzzy right now and I can't seem to pull that information from my brain. I'll sit here and think about it though and get back to you."

"Okay," Natasha said as she left the room.

About five minutes later, Doctor Lancer and Natasha walked back in. "Hello Camryn," Doctor Lancer greeted her with a smile.

"Hi Doctor Lancer, how are you?" Fendi asked.

"I'm doing great. I understand you're feeling a little under the weather?"

"Yes, I think I might be coming down with something."

"Yea, you're right about that."

"Why do you say it like that?" Fendi asked as she eyed the doctor suspiciously.

"Oh, well, I have a diagnosis for the way you've been feeling," the doctor said.

"Really? You haven't even examined me yet though."

"Sometimes, that's not necessary."

"What do you mean?"

"I mean, you're pregnant!" Doctor Lancer exclaimed as she clapped her hands. "Congratulations!"

Fendi looked from her to Natasha, as they both smiled like Cheshire cats. What the hell was Doctor Lancer talking about? She wasn't pregnant. She had just had an abortion four months ago. How could she be pregnant again so soon?

"What?" she asked in total shock and disbelief.

"You're going to have a baby," Doctor Lancer said.

"That can't be. Run the test again," Fendi said.

"We did. We always run them twice, just to be sure. Now, the only thing that's unclear is how far along you are. Natasha stated to me that you don't remember when your last menstrual cycle was. So, what I'm going to do is write you up a prescription for an ultrasound. You can take it to the imaging center on Bluebonnet. It's called Bluebonnet Imaging Center, which is the closest one to my office. They will perform an ultrasound and tell you how far along you are. I can also give you a prescription for some prenatal vitamins, but you're gonna want to get an Obstetrician as soon as possible. Do you have any other questions or concerns?"

Fendi was at a loss for words. She was dumbfounded by the information that Doctor Lancer had just given her. She couldn't even respond to her with words, so she just shook her head no. "Okay, well I'll write up the scripts and you can be on your way. Again, congratulations!! I'm so happy for you!"

The two women left the room and Fendi followed. She was absolutely stunned by this news. She was pregnant. She and Syd were having a baby. She retrieved the paperwork from the doctor and left the office in a daze. Once she got outside, she looked up at the sky and asked, "Why me, God? Why do you keep doing this to me?"

She got in her car and burst into tears. How could this be happening to her again? She and Syd weren't even together anymore and now, she was having his baby. She knew one thing for sure, she wasn't having an abortion this time. After the abortion, she felt sick for a while. Not because of the actual abortion, but because of what she had done.

She still had no regrets, because there was no way she was about to have a child by Tucker's gay and confused ass. She couldn't do that to a child. After she cried for a few minutes, she reached in the glove box for a tissue. She wiped her face and blew her nose before starting her car. She headed to the imaging center, because she needed to know how far along she was.

She gave the prescription to the receptionist and filled out a ton of paperwork. Finally, after thirty minutes, she was called to the back. She was taken to a room and was told to lay on the exam table, which was comfortable as hell. She relaxed and got comfy as they typed all her information in. The tech then asked her to raise her shirt and placed a paper over her bottom area.

She poured some cold gel on her tummy and began to move the warm wand over the gel on her belly. As she moved, she took measurements, then turned the screen to Fendi for her to look at what was on the monitor.

"This is your baby. You see the little heart beating?" the tech asked her with a smile on her face.

Fendi looked at the image and tears came to her eyes. She hadn't done this with the first pregnancy, because she didn't want anything to do with that baby. But, staring at the screen, with something that she and Syd created brought so many emotions to the surface. The tech grabbed a tissue and handed it to her. She thanked her and wiped her eyes with it.

"How far am I?" Fendi asked.

"Well, from the measurements I've taken, you seem to be about twelve weeks."

Fendi calculated in her head quickly just how far she was. Damn. She got pregnant right after the abortion. "So, I'm three months?"

"Yes, that would put your due date right around August 30th," she smiled.

"Oh wow!"

The technician printed out pictures of Fendi's ultrasound and handed them to her. She cleaned the gel off her stomach and said, "Have a great day and congratulations!"

"Thanks," Fendi said as she stared at the images of her baby.

As she walked out and to her car, she thought about how her actions last night could have caused her to miscarry. She vowed to never let a nigga or bitch put her in such a precarious situation again. She drove to the pharmacy to pick up the prenatal vitamins, then made her way home. When she turned the corner and saw Syd's car in the driveway, she rolled her eyes.

She got out the car and made her way to the front door, as if she never saw him. "So, you just gon' leave me standing out here wounded and shit?"

Syd wanted to just let Camryn go, but his heart wouldn't allow him to do that. "Syd, I don't feel well and wanna be left alone," she said with her back turned to him.

"You can't even look at me, Cam?" he asked.

She could hear the pain in his voice as he spoke, but she wasn't going to allow that to deter her from the decision she had already made.

"It's over, Syd. Just do you and I'll do me," she finally turned to face him with tears in her eyes. "I'm tired of the hurt and the pain that we keep causing each other. I'm tired of you cheating on me and trying to tell me how to live my life."

"But, we love each other. We can work this out, baby. Please," he begged.

"No, we can't. You want one thing and I want another and that will never work. I know we've broken up many times before this, but as God is my witness, this is the last time. I'm glad to see that you're okay, because I never meant to shoot you. But, you gotta let me go!" she said.

Tears streamed down her face and his, but she was done. She wasn't going to fight another bitch behind Syd ever again. She was going to be a mommy now and she had to do what was best for her child. If that meant letting go of the love of her life, so be it. She turned to walk in the house as Syd called after her. "Camryn! CAM! CAM, I LOVE YOU!" She just shut the door behind her and had herself a good cry.

Chapter One

Phoenix sat across from Jy, inside of Juban's, with her heart hanging to her knees. She was a nervous wreck, seeing that her husband was the only man she had been with for the past six years. Now that she was on a date, her nerves were frazzled, because this was all new to her.

"You good?" Jy questioned as his eyes landed on Phoenix, twirling her fork around in her shrimp and grits.

"Yeah, yeah, I'm fine. Just a bit nervous, I must admit." Jy nodded his head while taking a sip of water.

"Tell me a little about yourself, Ms. Phoenix." Phoenix dabbed the corners of her mouth with the napkin provided before sitting back in her chair.

"I'm thirty-two, no kids, and I'm soon to be divorced. That's about it honestly," she admitted before picking up her fork. She avoided eye contact, yet felt Jy's eyes watching her every move. "What about you?"

"Like I said before, my name is Jyri but everybody calls me Jy. I'm half Haitian, and I also have no kids. Never been married and don't plan on it anytime soon. I have a brother, but we're not as close as I wish we could be. My mother is deceased, three years now, and my pops is doing a bid upstate, so it's just me." Jy lustfully stared at Phoenix, causing her to blush slightly. Phoenix was smitten by Jy's biography and she wanted to learn more.

"Why are you single? Why don't you have any kids? What's up, because that shit ain't normal these days," she joked, cracking a smile.

"Nah it ain't, but I want to marry the mother of my child. I'm not trying to have baby mamas nor the drama that comes with it. I'm getting old and running behind bitches, knocking them up ain't in my plans. I see niggas every day, dogging different females and all that young nigga shit and I'm not for it. I'm looking for stability, a woman that can provide whenever I can't. Until I find that, I'd rather be by myself," Jy stated. Phoenix was deeply intrigued by Jy's response and the knowledge that he had just laid on a platter.

"Hmm, I can't argue with that. A man with sense, I like that," she confessed, grabbing her glass of water and taking a sip.

"Why the divorce?" he questioned, causing her to choke on her water. Patting her hand against her chest, Phoenix sat her glass back down and sighed.

"My husband was too controlling. He moved me out of Baton Rouge, promising me so much better yet things got worse. I eventually got tired and came back home and started dancing to provide stability for myself and he didn't like that. I begged and pleaded with him for another chance yet he wouldn't give me that. He constantly tried forcing a baby on me but I didn't want kids because I had dreams, I had my own thing I was trying to do. He went out and got another bitch pregnant and fucked my enemy, so here we are, at the drawing board conflicting on whether or not I should sue for alimony or just let it go. Don't get me wrong, I love that man with everything in me but he is not for me and I know that now." Jy's ears were wide open listening to Phoenix. He was shocked that a man could do such harm to a woman as beautiful as the one sitting before him, but he knew he had lucked out.

"That's deep. I'm sorry you had to endure that pain, baby girl. Love is a painful subject to talk about, especially when it's not real. It seems to me that your husband wasn't yours from the jump. He wanted to control your mind while abusing your heart. That shit is deadly, trust me; I already know about all that."

"And how is that?" I asked.

"I lived it more than once. My last girl left me for a nigga she thought was going pro. Five years I dedicated to that woman and she shitted on me the first chance she got. He fucked up his knee and the bid was out and she tried to come back, but I was done. You only have one time to fuck me over and I'm done." Jy raised his head and put his fork down. Phoenix was feeling Jy, no matter how hard she tried to deny it.

"I guess we both had our share of heartbreak, huh? My husband tried to come back, but I don't want all that baggage. His baby mama is young and dumb and I want no parts of whatever they have going on. He chose her the day he decided to get her pregnant and that there, will get your ass kicked to the curb real quick."

"Do you miss him?" he asked.

"I'm a real ass female with real ass feelings, so I won't sit here and say that I don't because I do, every day. But, I know being with him isn't healthy for me." Jy appreciated Phoenix's honesty as they continued to chat about different topics. Jy called for their tab and waited for the waitress. Once the tab was paid, he stood up from his seat and helped Phoenix to her feet. Walking out of the restaurant, they bumped right into the last person she thought she would see. Brazailia stood in front of Phoenix and Jy, with her hand resting on her hip and her lips twisted.

"Are you going to move or do I need to move your ass myself?" Phoenix questioned, preparing herself for a brawl. Her issue with Brazailia had nothing to do with Frederick. It was the fact that Brazailia was disrespectful to her and didn't know her place. Jy stood beside Phoenix with his hand on the small of her back, looking back and forth between the two women. He hated drama and he definitely hated the attention that it brought his way.

"Is everything aight, ma?" he asked Phoenix with his eyes still on Brazailia.

"Fine, perfectly fine. Let's go!" Phoenix walked around Brazailia, purposely bumping her shoulder. She knew with Brazailia being here, it only meant that Frederick was nearby and she definitely didn't want to see him. Walking full speed towards Jy's Lamborghini, Phoenix stood beside the door, tapping her feet while waiting for Jy to unlock the doors. Rage filled her insides, yet she tried to hold her composure. "I'm sorry about that. That was my husband's stupid ass baby mama and the sight of that woman pisses me off. I didn't mean to make a scene if I did. And, I'm sorry if I embarrassed you," Phoenix apologized. Jy started the engine and reversed out of the parking spot. He had a feeling Phoenix would be more to handle than he thought, yet he was willing to see what she was all about. There was something about her that just made him want to get to know her better. But, he still felt the need to give her a little insight as to who he was.

"You know, Phoenix, I want to get to know you better, which is why I invited you out tonight. But, my life is exactly how I want it to be, drama free. If you're over your ex, I think that the two of us might continue to see each other. But, if you're not quite over him yet and there are going to be instances like the one that just happened back there, I think I should walk away. I'm not in the habit of being anyone's second choice. I think you're beautiful, smart, feisty, and sexy as hell; exactly the kind of woman I need in my life, minus the drama. So, if you're not into me, I think you should let me know now. Another thing I don't like to do is waste my time," Jy said.

Phoenix was completely stumped when he said that. She didn't realize that she was making such an impression on him. She didn't like drama either, but somehow, it always seemed to follow her. Maybe it was time to take a leap of faith and try something new. After all, who wants drama following them for the rest of their life?

****

Syd stood outside of Fendi's door, feeling defeated and heartbroken. He couldn't imagine Fendi being serious about their relationship being over, but he knew he would have to deal with it. How was it that she was this mad at him when she was the one that shot him? With slumped shoulders and puffy red eyes, Syd walked back towards his car and got in. As bad as he wanted to beat Fendi's door down, he decided against it because he knew she wouldn't hesitate shooting him again. He loved Fendi and he knew that she loved him, but she was right; their love was toxic and he didn't see it getting any better.

Starting his engine, Syd backed out of Fendi's driveway. He watched in his rearview mirror as he pulled off, making a promise to himself that it was the last time he would go to her home.

Fendi watched Syd out of her window as he pulled away from her house. She desperately wanted to open the door and scream for him to come back, but what good would it do? She had made up her mind that she was done. She had to let him go, for the sake of her sanity and her child. There was no way she could have this baby and be with Syd; their relationship was just too toxic.

She finally dried her eyes and got up from the floor. She made her way to the bathroom because she was in need of a shower. She turned the water on and stepped under the water, allowing the warm spray to cleanse away all her hurt and pain. She rubbed her stomach and promised to take care of this baby, because she really loved Syd. The two of them had always dreamed of having a little one. Syd said he wanted her to have a little girl, who would look just like her. She dreamed of having a son that would look like his daddy. No matter what she had, she was going to love and protect her child from anyone that could possibly cause him or her pain. Even if that meant she had to end things with Syd for good.

Once she was finished taking her shower, she stepped out and dried herself off. She stood in front of the mirror and looked at her shapely body. She hadn't noticed it before, but she did have a little pooch in her belly. She knew that it would get bigger before it got smaller. She smiled at the fact that she was going to have a baby. She rubbed her belly, over and over again, smiling as she thought about the tiny being that was inside her. She moisturized her damp skin with her favorite lotion, then got dressed. She had a lot of planning to do and changes to make.

The first thing she knew she had to do was quit working at the club. Before she could pick the phone up to make the call, it began to ring. She looked at it and saw that it was Dollar calling her. She smiled because that was perfect timing.

"Hello," she answered.

"Fendi, I need you to come in as soon as possible…"

"Dollar, I quit!"

"What the fuck you mean you quit?! You just begged me to give you your fuckin' job back! I need you to get your ass over here right now!" he yelled angrily.

That was the type of shit Fendi didn't like. For a man who needed his dancers, he acted like they needed him. Fendi had plenty of money, so she didn't need to strip in no club. Now that she was pregnant, there was no way she was going to go twist her ass up on that stage with her little one resting in her belly. What kind of mother would she be if she did that?

"I'm not coming down there ever again. I SAID I QUIT!"

"IF YOU DON'T BRING YOUR FUCKIN' ASS DOWN HERE AND GET ON THAT STAGE…" Dollar was livid and she could tell by the way he was speaking to her.

"FUCK YOU, DOLLAR! YOU AND THAT RATCHET MUTHAFUCKIN' CLUB! I HOPE YOU

NEVER MAKE ANOTHER PENNY IN THAT BITCH ASS CLUB!" she yelled back and ended the call.

After she did that, she blocked his number from her phone, because she didn't need that kind of stress in her life. She had a baby on the way and because it was Syd's baby, there was no way in hell she was going to do anything to jeopardize her pregnancy. She wiped a lone tear from her cheek at the thought of Syd not being here to share in this moment with her.

"Don't worry, munchkin. I am going to do any and everything to protect you. I love your daddy and he loves me. He's going to love you, too. I'll tell him about you one day, but for right now, I'll just hold on to this little secret."

Fendi knew she was wrong for keeping this pregnancy from Syd, but she wasn't about to be caught up in all his bullshit. When he would be ready to stop playing these childish games, then they could try to work things out. She loved Syd more than any man she had ever dated. He was the one that stole her heart. She remembered everything about the first time they met, their first date, their first kiss… everything.

She climbed into bed and just embraced sleep. She was absolutely exhausted from her day. She hoped that tomorrow would be a better day.

Chapter Two

Hennessy was still feeling some kind of way about the way Syd left her at the movie theater that night. Two weeks had passed since that night and she was still pissed. She couldn't believe he did her dirty like that. She just couldn't understand what the fuck he saw in Fendi that made her so damn special. As far as Hennessy could tell, she wasn't shit. She was still trying to figure out how her plan to get back at Fendi backfired. Syd seemed all into her, but as soon as he saw Fendi, he just punked out.

Hennessy kept trying to figure out how to get revenge on everybody that wronged her, but she couldn't figure things out. She knew one thing, she wanted to burn down Dollar's damn club. She hated him with a passion and she knew the way to get to him was in his pockets. If she burned the club down, Dollar would never make another penny. That would be hitting him where it hurt the most.

Dollar had definitely done her wrong and she wasn't taking his disrespect lightly. She hated Dollar and the ground that he walked on. As she contemplated her next move, her mind began to get the best of her. She plotted on her revenge against Fendi, Vicious, Dollar, and even Syd for leaving her at the movie theater.

"That bastard," she cussed to herself.

Her phone rang and she checked to see who it was. It was her mom, so she answered.

"Hey mom."

"Hey baby, how are you doing?"

"I'm okay."

"Are you sure?"

Hennessy wondered why her mom was asking that question. What did her mom know that she didn't?

"I'm positive, mom, why are you asking?" Hennessy asked.

"Well, I've just been hearing some things so…"

"Some things? Some things like what?"

"Well, Ruth said she was in the store a couple of weeks ago and saw you fighting with some woman. I said, not my daughter. I know how Ruth can be nosy with a side order of messy, so I just knew she wasn't telling me the truth. I know that's not true, is it baby?"

"Mom, you really shouldn't listen to Miss Ruthie. She just talks a lot of mess," Hennessy said.

"Yea, that's the same thing I said. But then, she told me that you got arrested."

Hennessy rolled her eyes upward. She couldn't believe that people were sticking their noses in her business. She hadn't even seen Miss Ruthie in the store that day. She must have been hiding so she could get the scoop on Hennessy to go make mess.

"Mom, don't you worry about nothing Miss Ruthie says. You know ever since her husband left her for that young girl, she's had a lot of time on her hands. She's just feeding you some bull, so don't believe her."

"Well, I didn't want to believe her, but once she showed me the video,"

"Video? Oh my God, mom, what video?" Hennessy asked nervously.

"Dontchu worry about what video. Why didn't you tell me any of this shit?! Do you know how embarrassing it was for me to hear Ruth ask me if you was out of jail yet?"

My mom was always worried about the stuff people said about her and her family. When Hennessy first started dancing, she didn't know how to tell her mom. As it turned out, she didn't need to worry about that. Soon after she started stripping, her mom called and went off on her. Miss Ruth had ran her mouth to her mom already. She had rolled her eyes and wished sometimes Miss Ruth would just keep her mouth shut.

She couldn't take that the woman always ran to tell her mom everything. She couldn't understand what it was that made her constantly wanna divulge her information. She decided that maybe it was time to pay Miss Ruth a visit, as soon as she ended the call with her mom.

"Mom, I'm sorry I didn't tell you. I was embarrassed by it myself and wanted to keep it to myself."

"You were fighting in a grocery store with a woman over her husband? Didn't I raise you better than that? What kind of shit is that?! You're a smart woman and need to stop stooping to those levels. Why would you do some stupid shit like that?" Her mom was really giving it to her.

"I'm sorry mom. What more do you want me to say?"

"You don't have to say anything else! I just want you to stop making a fool of yourself!"

"Okay. Thanks mom. I realize that I'm a huge disappointment to you. You've made that very clear. Thanks... thanks so much!"

Hennessy was tired of her mom ragging on her about what she should and shouldn't do. It was like she just couldn't please her. In her eyes, she was doing what she needed to do for herself.

"Don't expect me to apologize to you for..."

"I'll talk to you later, mom. I have somewhere I need to go."

With that being said, Hennessy ended the call with her mother. She was steaming from the fact that Miss Ruth was constantly talking about her. She just wished the woman would mind her business. She had so many other things she could talk about, but she made Hennessy her main topic. She was tired of it. She grabbed her purse and slipped into her shoes.

She walked out to her car and made her way to Miss Ruth's house. If the bitch had something to say about her, let her say it to her face. That was how Hennessy felt and what she was feeling on the drive there. The whole ride there, Hennessy's hand was itching to ball up and punch something. She decided she would wait until she got to Miss Ruth's house to touch her messy and nosy ass.

Hennessy sat outside of Miss Ruth's home, biting her nails nervously. She was adamant on getting her point across to the nosy ass woman, yet she was all against disrespecting her elders.

"Fuck this!" She snapped, opening her car door with one foot out. As if she had forgotten everything that her mother had taught her, Hennessy stepped out of her car and stormed towards Miss Ruth's door. She beat on the door as hard as she could.

"I know your nosy ass in there, open the door!" she hissed.

Miss Ruth swung her door open with a grimacing expression adorning her face. With her hand on her hip, she sized Hennessy up and down. She was wondering what the little Trollip wanted with her. Hennessy wasn't a regular at Miss Ruth's. As a matter of fact, Ruth couldn't remember when was the last time she had a conversation with the young woman.

"Child, where are your manners? What the hell are you banging on my damn door for?" Miss Ruth asked with an attitude.

"The same reason your old ass stays in my business, why the hell are you so nosy? I had every intention to whoop your old ass, but looking at you right now, I see you're just a miserable old hag. You had no right to tell my mother anything about me! I'm a grown ass woman and my business should stay my damn business!" Hennessy attempted to step forward, but Miss Ruth pulled out her pepper spray and raised it so that Hennessy could see it.

"Don't make me use this on you, child. You should be ashamed of yourself for the way you out here tarnishing your good family's name. Now, Miss Ruth is saved, but I won't mind pulling out my 9mm if I feel threatened. Are you threatening me, lil girl?" Miss Ruth asked as she gave Hennessy a menacing stare. Hennessy didn't respond with words. She stood there twisting her lip upward, because as much as she wanted to snatch the messy ol' lady, she was not about to get killed for it. She knew that Miss Ruth wasn't lying about pulling out her piece.

"Go on home and meditate before your mother has to buy a new black dress to attend her daughter's funeral." Miss Ruth then stepped back and smirked before slamming the door in Hennessy's face. Hennessy felt like a fool for coming to Miss Ruth's house, but she felt even more stupid for allowing an old woman to put her in her place. Feeling embarrassed and defeated, Hennessy walked back towards her car and got in. She found herself punching the steering wheel repeatedly, hoping it would soothe her pain. The mere thought of failing crossed her mind causing a few tears to fall down her face.

Chapter Three

Camryn sat inside of her classroom going over Friday's spelling test. She was nauseated and having abdominal pains, yet she tried her hardest to ignore it.

"Miss Peters, these were left at the front desk for you," Mrs. Richardson stated, holding a small edible arrangement full of pineapples, honeydew, and grapes; Camryn's favorite fruits. Camryn grilled the arrangement as she walked over, grabbing them from Mrs. Richardson's hands. She then searched for a card that would expose who it was from, but she found nothing. Shrugging her shoulders, Camryn stepped back.

"You can have it, I don't want it."

"Really?" Mrs. Richardson questioned with a shocked expression. Camryn nodded her head and took her seat back at her desk. As soon as her bottom touched the seat, her phone vibrated in her desk. She grabbed her phone and opened the text message.

Tucker: Hope you liked the edible arrangements. I miss us Camryn.

Camryn: Nope, I trashed that shit. Goodbye.

She blocked Tucker's number and slammed her phone down. Massaging her temples, Camryn sat back in her seat and exhaled. Thoughts of Syd crossed her mind and she tried her hardest to remove them. She was missing him something awful, yet she knew she had to remain strong. She wanted nothing more than to feel him inside of her, seeing that her hormones were raging out of control with the pregnancy.

"Shit!" she hissed lightly, clenching her legs together, feeling the moisture in the crotch of her panties.

The bell rang for dismissal and Camryn couldn't have been happier. She was hungry, horny, and sleepy, and that combination caused rage to fill her insides. Fumbling through her Lauren Ralph Lauren tote for her keys, she headed towards her Benz. Once inside, she shifted in her seat in an effort to ignore the feeling of her secretions seeping through her lace boy shorts. Camryn started her engine and headed home to take a much needed cold shower.

Camryn pulled into her driveway and twisted her face once she saw Syd's baby mama sitting on her porch.

"I don't have time for this shit!" she said out loud as she parked her car. With her hand rested on her .22, Camryn exited her car and trotted towards the front door. Ursula stood from the porch, dusted the back of her too small shorts and raised her hands.

"I come in peace," she said before Camryn could get a word out.

"Hmmph, why the change of heart?" Camryn asked. She was a bit leery about the girl being at her home.

"Listen, Sydney doesn't know I'm here, so I will make this quick. The night I sent you those pictures, I drugged him." Camryn was two seconds away from beating the bitch down again. She had a lot of nerve coming here on some bullshit like that.

"And why the fuck would you do that?" Camryn asked.

"Because, I wanted that old thing back. I wanted us back and I thought I stood a chance. But, he had made it clear that he didn't want me and that he loved you and I overreacted. He never looked at me the way he looks at you. He never loved me the way he loved you. Hell, I don't even know if he ever did love me, so I can admit that I was jealous. I don't know what's going on between you two, but it's taking a fucking toll on him. I caught that nigga crying last night and that ain't Syd. I've never seen him cry for anything or anyone. I love Syd so much that I would sacrifice my happiness for his. I want to be the grown woman I should have been in the first place. If you love Syd as much as he loves you, can't you guys work it out?" Camryn's heart smiled at hearing Ursula tell her such things, but the fact still remained that she and Syd would never work.

"I appreciate you coming over and everything, but our problems are bigger than just you. We can't be together without hurting each other, so I threw in the towel. I just can't…"

"No offense, but if I would have shot that nigga, Junior wouldn't have his mother alive right now. Take heed of all the signs, that nigga loves you, girl." Ursula then stepped down from the porch and started to walk off. She turned around and smiled at Camryn.

"Oh yeah, congrats on the baby. I'll let you tell him," Ursula said.

"How did you…"

"You're too calm for one. I was almost afraid to come here because I thought you would whoop my ass again. But I had to come. I had to try to make this right.

Only a pregnant bitch would stay calm while the baby mama gives her advice on her relationship. Besides, you have a glow in your face that tells it all. Like I said, I'll respect you enough to let you tell him." Ursula got into her Toyota Corolla and pulled off, leaving Camryn sulking in her thoughts. She loved Syd with every fiber of her being, but she had to do what she had to do.

She couldn't allow her feelings for him to interfere with her trying to protect their unborn child. Maybe once she had the baby, she and Syd would be able to work things out. But, for right now, she had to do what was best for her during her pregnancy. Stupid ass Tucker wasn't making things no better, with his begging ass. After Ursula left, Camryn heard a car in her driveway. She didn't want to deal with anybody, so she closed her eyes and prayed that it wasn't about to be no bullshit.

Her doorbell rang and she inhaled, then quickly exhaled. She pulled the door back to come face to face with Drew. Now, this was some shit she wasn't expecting. Drew had never come to her house so she was definitely confused as to what he was doing there now.

"What the hell are you doing here, Drew?" she asked.

"I need to talk to you. May I come in?" he asked. He looked around nervously as he began to perspire.

"HELL NO! What the fuck are you doing at my house?"

"Look, my wife found some credit card charges on our billing statement," he said.

"So… what the hell does that have to do with me?" Camryn asked as she crossed her arms over her chest.

"She's on her way over here!" he said nervously as he continued to look around.

"Over here?! What the fuck she on her way over here for?!"

"I kinda told her that we were having an affair and that the charges, hotel charges, were from our stays there," he said.

"THE FUCK! Are you out of your fuckin' mind?!"

"I didn't know what else to tell her," he said in a panicked state.

Camryn was pissed, because although she and Drew were fooling around before, she had never gone to any hotel with him. She knew that must have been where he was going with Tucker when they were screwing. She was about to rip this nigga a new asshole.

"Wait a fuckin' minute! Are you telling me that you told your wife that the two of us were having an affair and that hotel charges she found were from the two of us?" she asked with her right hand posted on her hip.

Drew could see how pissed Camryn was and hoped that she wouldn't rat him out to his wife. It was best if his wife thought he was fucking a woman than telling her the truth about him and Tucker. There was no way he was going to confess some shit like that to her. He knew that if she did, his career would be over.

"Yea, I had to tell her something. She was…"

"Hold up, muthafucka! You would want to call your wife and tell her not to fuckin' come over here. I swear, if she comes here, trying to go off on me because of some shit you said, I will tell her the truth!"

"You can't! You can't tell her the truth. I'll lose everything and my career will be over!" Drew said.

"I don't give a fuck about you, your wife or your fuckin' career! That woman is not going to come over to my house and start some shit with me behind your ol' doo doo dick! Fuck that!" Camryn said angrily.

"Camryn please! If you do this for me, I'll give you a raise," Drew offered.

"Fuck a raise! You better call your wife!"

"Camryn…"

"Call your wife or I will tell her the truth," she said.

Camryn was standing firm in her position. There was no way she was going to allow Drew and his wife to fuck up her career, especially now that she was pregnant. Because she was having a baby, she wasn't going to the club to strip anymore. She needed the stability of her teaching career to keep her money rolling in. There wasn't going to be any lying on her part.

A few minutes later, she heard a car pulling up in her driveway. She hoped that it was Syd and not Drew's wife. The last thing she wanted was a confrontation with that woman. She didn't need any stress with her pregnancy.

She looked at Drew as his eyes grew big with fright.

BANG! BANG! BANG!

"OPEN THE FUCKIN' DOOR, BITCH! I SEE MY HUSBAND'S CAR IN YOUR DRIVEWAY!" yelled Drew's wife from the other side of the door.

BANG! BANG! BANG!

"You better get ready, because the shit is about to hit the fuckin' fan!" Camryn said as she walked towards the door to let his wife in.

As soon as she opened the door, WHAP! Drew's wife slapped her across the face.

"You fuckin' home wrecking bitch!" his wife said through clenched teeth.

Chapter Four

Syd had been feeling like he was dying since Camryn had told him it was over. He wanted nothing more than to go to her and make things right, but he knew she needed some space. He missed her more than words could say, but he didn't know what he could do to get her to take him back. He didn't know how he could make her see that he was in it for the long haul. He was sitting down on the sofa, watching Ursula play with their son.

He had found an apartment and had moved in with his son a week ago. Camryn was right when she said that if he loved her, he shouldn't have been staying with Ursula. He was just looking for a place to crash temporarily. He didn't want to get his own place because he planned on moving back in with Camryn. But, since she had ended things permanently, he didn't have a choice but to get his own place.

Ursula had wanted to come by for a play date with their son, so he let her. As long as he was around to supervise, he was cool with it.

"So, have you heard from your girl lately?" Ursula asked.

Syd gave her a look that said he didn't want to talk about it. She looked at him with a smirk on her face and said, "I was just asking because I know how much you love her. Look, I don't think I apologized to you for those pics, but I'm sorry. I was wrong and I should never have crossed that line. I guess I just didn't realize how much you loved her."

"Why don't you just spend time with Junior and stop worrying about what's going on in my business," Syd said.

"I just wanted to apologize. I hope that the two of you work things out."

"Whatever."

The last thing Syd wanted to do was discuss his business with Camryn with Ursula. For all he knew, she was just trying to see how vulnerable he was so she could swoop in for the kill. He was not going to give her any leverage.

"Mommy, when are you and daddy going to get back together so we can be a family?"

Syd rolled his eyes as he listened to the answer that Ursula would give to Junior.

Ursula pulled him onto her lap and kissed him on the cheek. "Baby, I need you to know that mommy and daddy love you very much. You know that right?"

"Yes," Junior answered in a soft voice.

"But, mommy and daddy are better off as friends. Do you know what that means?"

"It means that you and daddy are friends, like me and Lexi from across the hall."

"That's right. Even though we love you, we can't get back together," Ursula said.

"But why? Don't you love him?"

Ursula loved Syd very much, but she wasn't going to keep making a fool of herself by chasing a man who didn't want her. She now knew and understood how much he loved Camryn and as much as it hurt her, she had to stop fighting her feelings for him.

"I love your daddy, but he's better as my friend."

"Okay. Daddy?"

"Yea son," Syd said with a raised eyebrow.

"Do you still love mommy?"

"I love mommy because she gave me you."

"You don't want to be with mommy anymore?" Junior asked again.

"No, son. Like mommy said, we're better off as friends."

"Are you still gonna be with that mean lady?"

Syd watched as Ursula's eyebrows went up. "What mean lady are you talking about, baby?" Ursula asked.

"The mean lady that daddy was living with."

"Was she mean to you?" Ursula asked as she glared at Syd.

"Yea. She yelled at me for watching TV when I was eating," Junior said.

"WHAT?!"

"Yea, and she yelled at me because she didn't want me on her white rug."

Ursula was pissed now. She didn't know that Camryn had been mean to her son. She couldn't understand why Syd kept something so important from her, but she was about to find out.

"Junior, can you go to your room so mommy can talk to daddy for a minute?" she asked.

"Okay," he said as he took off running to his room.

She jumped up from the floor and asked, "What the hell Syd?!" Ursula stood with her arms folded and her nostrils flared in anger.

"Man don't start that dumb shit because I will put you the fuck out. I already handled Camryn and told her to watch how she talks to him. Camryn is just a little bit aggressive, she didn't mean any harm when she said the shit. I don't…"

"And then you're sitting here taking up for the bitch. I should go over there and beat her stupid ass. Here I was trying to make amends with this stripper ho' and she was mistreating my son." Syd jumped up and rushed Ursula, snatching her by the collar of her shirt. With dark eyes and heavy breathing, he looked at Ursula with nothing but disgust in his eyes.

"I thought I made myself clear when I told you to watch your fucking mouth when you speak on her. I said I handled it so leave the shit alone." He released her. "Besides, you know like I know that you can't beat her ass. She already tore you a new asshole, so don't try no dumb shit. GET THE FUCK OUT MY SHIT!" he demanded before walking away. Ursula straightened out her clothes before calling Junior.

"JUNIOR! LET'S GO!"

Syd looked at her as if she had two heads.

"I told you to get out, my son stays here," he spat, taking a seat on his leather loveseat. Ursula snatched her Michael Kors knock off tote and proceeded to walk out of the door.

"You're so stuck up that girl's ass that you don't even know when she's keeping a secret from your dumb ass. Good luck with that Sydney," With that said, Ursula exited Syd's home leaving him in deep thought.

"Keeping a secret from me? A secret about what?" he asked himself as he sat there alone trying to figure out what the hell Ursula was rambling about.

****

Camryn stepped back, holding her face while Drew held his wife back as she tried to attack her once more. Camryn just knew that bitch hadn't just put her damn hands on her.

"I know like hell this bitch didn't…" Camryn spat before reaching around Drew and punching his wife in her right eye. "Bitch, you have lost every inch of that small ass mind putting your hands on me. You have no idea how bad I want to fuck you up right about now," she ranted, considering the fact that she had a life growing inside of her.

"NO, YOU HAVE LOST YOUR MIND FUCKING MY HUSBAND AND THINKING I WOULDN'T FIND OUTABOUT IT!" Drew's wife tried her hardest to break free, but he held a tight grip on her. He felt like shit for allowing such drama to knock on Camryn's door.

"Drew, I'm telling you right now. You have five seconds to get this creature away from my got damn house or she will be the first bitch at the courthouse tomorrow."

Drew's neck snapped in Camryn's direction as his eyes begged for her not to expose him. He would do anything for her to keep her lips sealed.

"LET ME GO DREW… RIGHT NOW! THIS BITCH IS ABOUT TO FEEL IT! IT'S BITCHES LIKE YOU THAT FUCK UP MARRIAGES BECAUSE YOU CAN'T FIND YOUR OWN DAMN MAN. HE WOULDN'T EVEN TAKE YOUR HOMEWRECKING ASS TO A FIVE STAR HOTEL BITCH! YOU WEREN'T EVEN WORTH THAT!" She spat as she attempted to spit Camryn's way.

"Did you just try to spit on me?"

"I damn sure did, bitches like you deserve to be spit on. HOMEWRECKING ASS CAMRYN!"

Camryn stepped closer to Drew and his wife as she continued to tussle with him.

"That's it, fuck this shit! I don't have time for this shit and Drew, you let this shit happen! Let me tell your ol' dry pussy ass something ho', because you've been itching for it. You're your own homewrecker bitch and you wanna know why? Because you couldn't keep your man satisfied. You couldn't keep him interested. That shit between your legs must be damaged or rotten, because this nigga here done said hello to the other side," Camryn said with a smirk on her face.

"Other side? What the hell you mean other side?" Drew's wife asked.

"I mean, your husband wasn't at a hotel with me. Hell, he never was and I don't know why he told you that. He should have never involved me in your bullshit! You're over here acting a damn fool on the wrong bitch. His ass ain't even worried about a bitch like that, at all." Camryn folded her arms with a sinister smirk across her face. She had just dropped the bomb on Drew and she felt damn good about it.

She didn't care what he and Tucker did, as long as they kept her out of it. But now that he done put her in the mix, she was not about to go down like that. She wasn't about to keep that shit secret and have that bitch try and ruin her career with lies and bullshit.

Drew's wife stopped trying to fight him, so he released her.

"What are you insinuating exactly?"

"Girl, I know your ass has more sense than that, or am I wrong? Your husband is a damn QUEER, A FLAMING FAGGOT, BOOTY BANDIT, MUDDY BUDDY, or whatever the hell you want to call it."

"CAMRYN, SHUT THE FUCK UP!" Drew said as he back handed Camryn, causing her to stumble. Licking her lips, the taste of blood seeped through her teeth, which caused her to snap.

"I know the fuck you didn't just... you know what?" Camryn walked off into her kitchen and grabbed her .22 from her purse. She heard scuffles from the other room. When she neared the corner, Drew's wife was whooping his ass something serious. But, that did little to cheer her up. Drew's wife pushed Drew and dived to the floor as Camryn's finger squeezed the trigger.

POW!

One bullet hit Drew in the same arm that he had just hit her with. He yelped in pain as he looked at Camryn like she was insane.

"You crazy bitch!! Why would you shoot me?"

"Shoot you? Nigga, I'm about to kill you and that bitch. NOW, GET THE FUCK OUT OF MY GOTDAMN HOUSE!" she barked, raising her gun once more. She wasn't about to fight with Drew or his wife, regardless of how either of them felt. Her drama days were over the moment she found out she was pregnant with Syd's baby.

"Camryn, I apologize for bringing…"

"I don't want to hear that bullshit. Take your ass on and don't ever come back over here." Camryn slammed her door and watched as Drew made his way to his car while his wife continued to yell obscenities.

"Stupid ass bastard," she spat, walking away from her window. Walking into her kitchen, she grabbed a bottle of water and took a seat at her kitchen table. Syd had been on her mind heavy, but she tried to fight it. She missed his presence, she missed him inside of her, and most importantly, she missed the love that he gave. She wished wholeheartedly that they could get back together for the sake of their child, but she knew it was impossible. She was tired of fighting with Syd over shit that didn't matter. She didn't want to keep fighting with Ursula or any other female. It was time to grow up and get her life together and if it didn't include Syd, so be it.

Camryn's ringing phone drew her from her thoughts. Syd's number flashed across her screen and she couldn't hide the smile that had managed to form on her lips. She fought within herself on whether or not she wanted to answer. Just as the thought of answering crossed her mind, it quickly left. A lone tear slipped from her eyes as she realized that they were really over and it was killing her softly. No man had ever had an effect on her the way Syd had and she didn't know how to handle it. Standing up from her table, she retrieved her things and headed upstairs to take a quick nap. A slight headache had started and she hoped to get rid of it before it got any worse.

As soon as her foot hit the top step of the stairs, her doorbell rang, startling her. Camryn ran into her bedroom and looked out of the window to see Syd's car sitting in her driveway with the driver's door still open.

"Shit!"

Chapter Five

"Please Phoenix, just give us one more shot?" Frederick begged his wife to take him back and give their marriage another chance.

"Boy bye, you must got me fucked up if you think I'm finna try and make this bullshit of a marriage work. What was it you said when I asked you to work things out? Oh yea, you said that we were just too damn different and needed to move on. Do you remember that shit?" she asked as she stared at him with her arms across her chest.

"I was wrong. I should've never…"

"Shoulda, woulda, coulda… it don't matter no more. You filed for divorce, I signed the papers and in a month or so, we'll be free of each other."

"I don't wanna be free from you. I want to work it out," he said.

"Ain't nothing to be worked out. You moved on and so have I…"

"What? What do you mean you've moved on?"

Frederick was shocked to hear that Phoenix had moved on. Who the hell had she moved on with? He wasn't even aware that she was dating anyone. He had hoped that she was still pining over losing him and would be too happy to take him back. He missed Phoenix and the way his life used to be, before he started sleeping with Brazailia. He felt as if he was losing his mind being around her immature ass all the time.

He stayed because he knew the military would look down on him if they ever found out that he cheated on his wife. If there was one thing they didn't take lightly, it was infidelity. The military taught discipline, self-respect, and morals, so finding out that Frederick had not only cheated on his wife, but also gotten his side chick pregnant, not once but twice, could definitely get him dishonorably discharged.

He knew that he was taking a huge chance trying to get back with Phoenix. If she agreed, Brazailia might make good on her threats to rat him out to his captain. After she had caught him begging Phoenix to take him back the first time, she was livid. She told him that they had kids together and he needed to stay with her and marry her. When he told her that he was never going to marry her, because he was still in love with Phoenix, she threatened him. He remembered that day like it happened yesterday instead of two weeks ago.

"You bastard!" Brazailia yelled angrily. Frederick looked at her and was actually scared. She looked as if she was possessed and shit.

"Calm down and watch your tone," Frederick said in a calm voice. He didn't want to wake their baby.

"All this time I've been fighting to make this relationship with you work. Even though I've noticed you distancing yourself from me. I tried to tell myself that I was overreacting, but I wasn't, was I Fred?! You filed for divorce. We're having another baby! Why would you ask her to take you back now?!" she asked as her voice broke and tears slipped from her eyes. "I love you, Fred!"

"This isn't working for me. We're just too different. You're younger than I am and you're extremely immature. I just don't think I can ever be happy with you," Frederick responded. "Now, I'm really sorry if that hurts your feelings, but I'm still in love with my wife."

That was when shit really got ugly. It was like the demons that took over Carol Ann in Poltergeist now had Brazailia. She looked at Fred with such rage in her eyes, he thought that any minute, the demons were going to show themselves.

"You have feelings for HER?! YOU'RE STILL IN LOVE WITH HER?! AFTER EVERYTHING WE'VE BEEN THROUGH!" she cried.

"Yes, I'm sorry. I never meant to hurt you."

"YOU NEVER MEANT TO HURT ME?! ARE YOU FUCKIN' KIDDING ME RIGHT NOW?!"

"No, I'm not kidding and you need to lower your voice before you wake the baby. Also, getting too excited isn't good for you. You could go into premature labor," he said as he tried to get her to calm down.

"FUCK YOU, FRED! YOU GOT ME PREGNANT TWICE AND NOW YOU WANT TO LEAVE ME TO TAKE CARE OF THESE LIL BASTARDS BY MYSELF! THAT AIN'T GOING DOWN LIKE THAT, NIGGA!" she said.

That was the first time Frederick heard her refer to their children as bastards and he didn't like it one bit. So what if they weren't married? That didn't mean she had the right to disrespect his kids. The kids were innocent in all of this.

"You need to watch what you say about my kids!" Fred said.

"Watch what I say about my kids? I say what the fuck I want about my kids!"

"Those kids didn't ask to be here, but they are, so you need to stop calling my kids names!"

What I said about them being bastards is true! Are we married? NO! Do you want to marry me? NO! So, they are what they are and will remain that way until you marry me! But, you aren't going to do that, are you? BECAUSE YOU'RE STILL IN LOVE WITH THAT STRIPPER HO'!"

Frederick had heard enough. He couldn't hold back his anger anymore and just swung on her.

WHAP!

Brazailia was stunned at first, because that was the first time he had ever put his hands on her like that. But, she was from the hood, so she knew how to defend herself. So what if Fred was a man? He had put his paws on her and she was not about to let him get away with it. She jumped on him and started clawing and slapping him, even though she was seven months pregnant. At that moment, the only thing she saw was red and she was going to make that nigga bleed.

"Brazailia, stop it now!" Frederick said as he tried to block her blows.

He didn't want to swing on her in the state she was in, because he really didn't want to hurt her or the baby. He finally managed to grab her hands and stop her from hitting him anymore.

"Look, I'm sorry if I hurt you. I'll always be here for my kids and I'll take care of them too. I'm not just gonna walk out on them, but I can't do this shit with you no more! I can't live like this no more!" he tried to explain.

"Oh, trust me, I know you're not going to walk out on us. You wanna know how I know? Because, if you leave me, I will have no choice but to tell your captain about us," she sneered.

"What?" Fred was shocked that she would even take it there. Reporting that shit to his captain could get him kicked out of the military. That was his life and he wasn't about to have that happen.

"You heard me. I'm not about to be a single mother, so whatever you need to work out with yourself, you better do it and do it quickly! I'm not playing with you, Fred! Now, get the fuck off me!" she said as she wiggled her wrists out of his grasp.

Fred didn't even have a response for her. He just stood there, mouth gapped open, as she took a seat on the sofa and turned on the television. If Brazailia thought she was about to keep him miserable, she could forget that. He'd rather kill her first.

"Hello... hellllllooooo!" Phoenix said as she snapped her fingers in front of his face, bringing him back to the present.

"Oh, sorry. My mind just was thinking back to when we were happy. I want that for us again," Fred said.

"Look, you gotta go. My man about to pull up and I don't want him to get the wrong idea," she said as she walked over to the door to open it.

"Your man? You are still my wife, Candice!" he said.

Phoenix busted out laughing. She couldn't believe her "husband" was acting this way. All while she was moping around and wanting him back, he was nowhere to be found. But now that she had moved on, he wanted her back. Well, she wasn't having it and she was unbothered by his ass. All of a sudden, Frederick spotted the Lambo turning into his mother-in-law's driveway. He watched his wife get all excited and knew that must be her new man.

"Who the fuck is that?" he asked angrily.

"My man," she said. "Now, get on outta here. As you can see, I've moved on."

Fred had no intentions on going anywhere, at least not before he sized the dude up.

"Phoenix, you're into thugs now? I never took you to be the hoodrat type to chase niggas that don't even have a decent credit score. This has to be some type of sick joke. Baby, come on! You cannot be serious!"

Fred reached for Phoenix's hand, yet she snatched it away. There was no way in hell she would go anywhere with him after everything that he had put her through. Jy smirked at Frederick while rubbing his goatee.

"Now, the old me would be on your head about the smart remarks that you made when you don't know shit about me. I'm not into drama; it makes me miss out on my money. If my ears heard correctly, my lady here doesn't want to be bothered with your ass anymore. So why don't you go ahead and leave before shit gets ugly."

Frederick stepped away from Phoenix as she grabbed his arm, but he snatched it away. He walked closer to Jy as he continued to grill him.

"I'm from the streets, just like you. I'm not afraid of you or anyone else for that matter. This is my wife and she will remain just that…" Before Frederick could finish his sentence, Jyri had him by the collar of his shirt, tossing him out on his ass.

"I'm trying to remain as calm as possible, but you're making it really hard."

Phoenix sprinted off of her mother's porch and stood between the two. She had a hand on both of their chests as she tried to keep them from coming to blows in front of her mom's house.

"Frederick, you need to leave. We are in the process of getting a divorce, so I won't be your wife for too much longer. It's too late for all this shit. You chose what you wanted and now, there's no turning back. I'm fine where I am and I've accepted the divorce. Now, leave please!" Phoenix spat, pointing towards Frederick's car. Frederick grilled Jy before he stormed off towards his car and got inside. He flicked Jy off before he peeled out. Phoenix wrapped her arms around Jyri, embarrassed at what had just transpired.

"I'm so sorry about that, babe!"

Jyri lifted her chin and kissed her passionately.

"Everything is everything ma. That chapter is closed."

****

Once Syd pulled out of Camryn's driveway, she breathed a sigh of relief. It took everything in her not to open the door and kiss all over him. More than anything, she wanted to pour her heart out to him, but she knew she had to remain strong. Had anyone told her that love would have been this hard, she would have steered clear of it. After giving it much thought, she decided that it was time to start a brand new life and the first step would be relocating. Her home held too many memories of which she tried so hard to forget. Her life with Syd was nothing short of amazing, yet heartbreaking. She wanted to live peacefully, but she knew she couldn't as long as she remained in the home she currently resided in.

Taking a seat at her Hewlett-Packard computer, she powered it on and immediately started searching for a new place she could call home. Hurtful thoughts of what she and Syd shared over the years and the fact that their relationship was over for good, taunted her. Her heart ached each time she thought about the drama that surrounded her each and every time she had to defend what they had. Thoughts of Drew and his wife coming over to her home caused a mean scowl to grace her face.

"Ol' gay ass stupid bastard," she spat.

She couldn't believe that Drew had tried to pull a fast one on her, knowing the type of person she was. As she scrolled the common website, Trulia, she came across a nice, three-bedroom condo about thirty minutes away from her home. She was in awe of the interior, the high vaulted ceilings caught her attention immediately. Camryn jotted down the contact info and continued to scroll. After an hour of searching, she had three options that she decided to look into.

Camryn spent her Saturday calling agents in an effort to get a new place as soon as possible. Now that she had made the decision to move, she was anxious to do so. After the agent requested her presence for a showing, Camryn fled from her seat to get dressed. Taking a quick shower, she applied lotion to her body. Throwing on a pair of ripped jeans and a simple Armani Exchange t-shirt, she smiled, realizing that her belly was slowly protruding. Throwing her hair into a sleek ponytail, she slid on a pair of Valentino Garavani sandals. Once she grabbed her Henri Bendel bag, she headed out of the door.

****

"As you can see, the ceilings are high vaulted and it makes the scenery far more elegant if you stand at the top of the stairs and look over the banister. We get a lot of compliments on the cherry oak banister as well," the real estate agent said as she walked in front of Camryn. She was in awe of the entire floor plan. The condo was absolutely exquisite from the beautiful hard wood flooring to the sleek marble countertop in the kitchen. She was especially taken aback when she saw the gorgeous view of the lake behind the condo. There was water sprouting from the ground and even a wooden bridge to cross over to the other side. Without further hesitation, Camryn halted the agent's steps.

"I WANT IT!" she stated happily.

The smile on the agent's face was so huge, it reminded her of a kid at a Chuck E. Cheese birthday party. "Oh, I'm so glad to hear that and you won't regret it. Give me a call on Monday morning and all of the proper paperwork will be drawn up."

They shook hands to seal the deal and Camryn walked away, smiling from ear to ear. Being a new home owner had her extremely excited and to know that she would be in her new place by the time her baby arrived had her ecstatic. Camryn drove away, staring at her new home in her rearview mirror. She couldn't wait to tell Phoenix. Stopping at Han's Philly & Wings to grab something to eat, she got out of her car and slammed the door. She walked in with her head held high.

"Thank you for choosing Han's, what can I get for you today?"

"A Philly cheesesteak with extra cheese, no onions or bell peppers, extra mushrooms. I also want a ten piece order of wings, honey mild and a large peach punch."

She looked at me with a shocking expression.

"What you looking at?" Camryn snapped.

"Nothing, just a little shocked is all. You're so tiny. Sorry if I offended you," the clerk replied.

"Sorry for snapping at you. I'm just a little hungry."

Camryn walked away and waited for her food while playing Candy Crush on her phone.

"We meet again, huh?" Camryn looked up as Vicious stood before her. As if she hadn't heard anything Vicious said, she looked back down at her phone screen and continued to play her game. There was no way in hell she would waste another minute of her time on Vicious' triflin' ass. She didn't fuck with her, nor would she pretend as such.

"Order 51," the clerk said into the microphone. Camryn scurried to grab her food. From the way her stomach growled, she knew that her little one couldn't wait to eat, so she decided to dine in the restaurant. Once she got her food, she walked to her seat and sat down.

Closing her eyes, she silently prayed over her food then dug in, all the while keeping a close eye on Vicious. She didn't trust her and she would be damned if she got caught slipping. Devouring the Philly cheesesteak, Camryn took the napkin and dabbed the corners of her mouth as Vicious prepared to leave. She smirked at Camryn as she made haste out of the door. Shrugging her shoulders, she continued eating until there was nothing left. Grabbing her bag, she grabbed her trash and tossed it before making her way out of the door.

She walked out the door and headed towards her car, her butt twisting from side to side. Camryn headed home, shifting uncomfortably in her seat. She was full beyond words as she stopped at the nearest gas station. She walked inside and paid for gas and grabbed a blueberry slush. As she walked out, she dropped the slush in frustration as Vicious stood beside her car, dragging her keys along the side.

She couldn't believe the bitch had the audacity to not only follow her to the gas station, but to have the nerve to key her car, knowing that she was right inside. She immediately pulled out her phone and snapped a couple of pictures, then turned to the clerk and said, "Call the police please."

"Is there a problem, ma'am?" the clerk asked.

"That bitch is keying my car. Call the police, because she's about to get dealt with."

The clerk picked up the phone as Camryn walked outside. Vicious stood there smiling at what she had done to Camryn's precious BMW. Camryn looked at the damage that her rival had done to her vehicle and wanted to smack that stupid smirk off her face. But, due to the fact that she was pregnant, she spared her from that ass whooping she deserved. But, she wasn't going to let that heffa get away with the shit. Nah, Camryn had something special in store for her ass.

"You fuckin' stupid bitch!" Camryn spat; she was livid. "You keyed my fuckin' car! Do you know how much that shit is about to cost your ass?!"

"It ain't about to cost me shit, bitch! It will however, probably cost you a pretty penny or two," Vicious smirked as she admired her handiwork. She was so proud of herself, because she had gotten under Fendi's skin without even touching her.

Camryn stood there shaking in her expensive sandals, because she was so pissed. She had to think this through, because she was carrying a child. She couldn't fight the bitch, because she might miscarry. She couldn't shoot her because then she'd get arrested. Sure, the charges might get dropped for self-defense, but she didn't want to spend a minute behind bars. She reached in her handbag as she walked closer to Vicious, who was smiling like a Cheshire cat.

"I just thought you would like your car better with pinstripes," Vicious smiled.

"Oh yea," Camryn smiled, which should have alarmed Vicious, had she been paying attention. "Well, maybe your face will look better on fire." Camryn pulled out the tobacco sauce pepper spray and began to spray Vicious all over her face. Vicious screamed like a wounded cat from the intense pain as the liquid continued to hit her face; eyes, nose and mouth.

Sirens could be heard coming up the street, so Camryn stopped and placed the small canister back in her handbag. Vicious continued to scream, "YOU STUPID BITCH! HELP ME! GET SOME WATER OR SOMETHING!"

Camryn laid eyes on the gas pump that was waiting to be used. At the same time she picked up the nozzle, the police pulled into the parking lot. "You just got saved, bitch. I was about to make a torch outta yo triflin' ass!" Camryn said as she opened the gas tank of her car and stuck the nozzle in it. Vicious continued to scream as the police ran up on the two of them.

"Dispatch, we need paramedics to 2728 Corral Whip Drive."

"What happened here?" the officer asked.

"THAT BITCH MACED ME WITH PEPPER SPRAY!" Vicious yelled.

Camryn had finished pumping her gas, so she removed the nozzle and placed it on the hook. "Ma'am?" the officer looked at her for an explanation.

"Officer, I did mace her but I was defending myself and my property. I went in to get gas and on my way out, that woman was keying my car. See," she showed the officer a picture of Vicious keying her car. "When I confronted her, she approached me in a combative manner and since I'm pregnant," she said as she cradled her small baby bump. "I had no choice but to defend myself."

"SHE'S LYING! I DIDN'T DO ANYTHING! SHE JUST BEGAN SPRAYING THAT PEPPER SPRAY IN MY FACE!" Vicious yelled. "DO SOMETHING, SHIT! MY FUCKIN' EYES ARE ON FIRE!"

"Officer, I'm not lying and I have a witness. The clerk inside the store saw everything," Camryn said.

"Hey, aren't you a dancer at Club Lush?" the officer blushed as he looked at Camryn. Clearly, he was a fan. She rolled her eyes at the fact that he recognized her as a dancer at the strip club. All she wanted was to leave that life behind her and start fresh.

"I'm actually not in that line of work anymore," she smiled. No need to piss off the cop when she could use his obvious crush to her advantage. "Are you going to arrest her for damaging my car? That is going to cost me a lot of money to fix."

"No, it won't. Once I fill out the paperwork, you can use it to file a claim," he smiled at Camryn. He then turned his attention to Vicious and barked, "You are under arrest for malicious destruction of property and attempted assault. Please place your hands behind your back!"

"PLACE MY HANDS BEHIND MY BACK? UNDER ARREST? DO YOU NOT SEE MY FUCKIN'

FACE?!" Vicious yelled angrily. She couldn't believe that the cop was arresting her after Fendi had sprayed her in the eyes with pepper spray. Her eyes were literally on fire; they were burning and blurry. She could barely see out of them and was worried she might have permanent damage.

"Please, put your hands behind your back, ma'am. Don't make this harder than it has to be!" the cop told Vicious in a tone that let her know he wasn't playing. She did as she was told as she tried to make out Camryn's face through her fucked up eyes.

"I CAN'T BELIEVE YOU'RE ARRESTING ME?! I'M THE VICTIM HERE, MUTHAFUCKA!" she yelled as the ambulance pulled in. "FENDI, HELP ME… PLEASE!"

"You have the right to remain silent. If you give up that right…" the police officer said.

"YOU CAN'T ARREST ME! SHE MACED ME! I'M THE DAMN VICTIM!" Vicious repeated.

"If you give up that right, anything you say, can and will be used against you in a court of law. You have the right to an attorney. If you cannot afford an attorney, one will be appointed for you by the courts."

The cop dragged Vicious over to the awaiting ambulance and waited as they tended to her face. He came back over to Camryn and said, "I'm going to need you to make a statement and I need to take pictures of your car."

"Yea, sure."

He pulled out a camera and began to take pictures of the scratch marks on Camryn's car. "She really did a number on your car," he said.

"Yea, but as long as I get a copy of that police report from you, I can get it fixed in no time."

"Oh, don't worry. I'll have it ready for you within the next two or three days," he promised.

"Thank you, Officer O'Malley," Fendi said as she read the name badge on his shirt.

Once he was finished taking pictures, he handed Fendi a report so she could fill in everything that happened. She completed the paperwork at the same time the paramedics said they were done with Vicious.

"Thank you, ma'am. Just call the station in about three days and we'll have the incident report done for you," the officer stated. He then turned his attention to Vicious and said, "Let's go!"

"Wait! Can't you see I'm injured?! I need to go to the hospital!" she cried.

"Ma'am, there's nothing they can do for you at the hospital that we haven't done here," the paramedic said.

"Am I free to go?" Camryn asked Officer O'Malley.

"Oh yes ma'am. Enjoy the rest of your day," he said with a huge smile on his face. He couldn't believe he got to talk to the beautiful Fendi. He was going to make sure he did everything possible to get Vicious' ass prosecuted.

He hauled Vicious off from the ambulance and threw her in the back seat of the squad car. Vicious watched Fendi get in her car and flipped her off before the officer drove out of the parking lot. She couldn't understand what it was about that bitch that was so special that men were literally falling for her.

Chapter Six

Syd sat in his recliner, slouched down while tossing back Colt 45s, tuned in for Monday night football. As hard as he tried to focus on what was playing on the TV, his mind constantly drifted off to Camryn. He missed her something serious and it was killing him that he hadn't seen or talked to her. Three months had passed and each day was far more dismal than the last. His heart broke each day that passed and he was slowly losing his sanity. It didn't make it any better that he popped up on several occasions and she never opened the door once.

"How long are you going to sulk in your misery behind that damn girl? It's been months, this house is a damn mess, and your ass is starting to smell. You need to get up and get it together Sydney," Ursula stated as she walked in and snatched the remote out of his hand. She then turned off the television while Syd laid back as if she hadn't said a thing.

"Not today Ursula. I'm not in the fucking mood."

"You've been saying that for months now and Junior notices the way you've been acting every single day. When are you going to realize that it's over between you and her, and move on with your life?" she asked. She was overwhelmed with the way Syd was carrying on, but she was partially jealous that he never showed her a care in the world.

"I know it man, but this shit hurts. She won't even fucking talk to a nigga and tell me what we can do to fix it. I love that girl, Urs," Syd admitted. Ursula shifted her body, feeling a bit uneasy. "What's that about?"

"What?" she asked, trying to throw him off the subject.

"You acting all weird and shit. Just get out, man. You ain't gotta worry about me; I'll be aight. Take Junior with you," he requested.

"HELL NO! YOU WANTED HIM, SO YOU GOT HIM! Get your shit together, Syd and do it quick!"

"JUST DO WHAT THE FUCK I SAID AND TAKE JUNIOR WITH YOU!" he spat, feeling his anger spiraling out of control.

"YOU WILL NOT YELL AT ME LIKE THAT, NIGGA! WHO THE FUCK YOU THINK YOU TALKING TOO?! I'M OVER HERE WORRIED ABOUT YOU AND THAT BITCH DON'T GIVE TWO FUCKS ABOUT YO ASS. YOU WANTED JUNIOR, SO NOW YOU GOT HIM. IT'S TOO LATE TO BE A DAMN DEADBEAT SINCE YOU OUT HERE MAKING BABIES AND SHIT!" she spat right back at him. Realizing what she had said, Ursula immediately grabbed her mouth as Syd rose from his seat.

"The fuck you just say?"

"Nothing, just forget it. I'll take Junior with me." Ursula grabbed Junior's hand and swiftly made her way to the door. As soon as she opened the door, Syd slammed it, almost smashing her hand in the process.

"Repeat what you just said, Ursula. I'm not fucking playing." Syd's eyes caused fear to surface inside of Ursula, so she wasted no time throwing Fendi under the bus.

"Camryn is pregnant."

"Pregnant? Quit lying!"

"I ain't lying!" Ursula said.

"How? I mean, how do you know that shit?" he inquired. "Ain't no way she would be sharing no shit like that with yo ass."

"I went to her house a few months back and that was when I found out. I was gonna tell you that day, but she begged me not to. I told her that I would give her the opportunity to tell you, but…"

Syd swung the door open, leaving Ursula and Junior standing there. He was livid and he needed answers. Ursula knew she had stuck her foot in her mouth, but she knew there was no turning back. Hell, she had no regrets about telling Syd that Camryn was pregnant. Shit, Camryn should have told him herself. Then, she wouldn't have had to say anything. Oh well, what's done is done.

****

"You can set that sofa down right over there," Camryn said as she directed the movers as they walked in carrying her furniture. It was finally moving day for her and she was exhausted, but excited at the same time. She hadn't eaten anything besides a bag of potato chips and her little one was wreaking havoc inside of her uterus.

"That's it, Ms. Peters, we've brought all of your furniture in and positioned them where you requested. Is there anything else we can help you with?" one of the movers questioned.

"No, I believe I can take it from here. Thank you so much," she replied, handing the three men two hundred dollars apiece. Once they walked out, Camryn sat down on her sofa, unbuckled her pants, kicked off her shoes and picked up her feet. She looked around and admired her new home. She had so many ideas on how she would decorate it that her head was spinning. Her doorbell rang and she got up to answer it. Knowing it was Phoenix, Camryn swung the door wide open with a bright smile.

"You would come when a bitch doesn't need any more help. That's how black folks do," she cackled as they embraced each another.

"I'm sorry, I was waiting on Jy's slow ass." Phoenix looked towards the driveway as Jyri stepped out and walked towards the door. Camryn smiled and looked at her best friend, giving her an approving nod. In her eyes, Phoenix had done a huge upgrade from Frederick. Jyri's thuggish demeanor was quite appealing and the complete opposite of Frederick.

"Babe, this is my best friend Camryn; Camryn this is Jy."

Jy extended his hand and Camryn shook it.

"Nice to meet you," she said.

"Likewise," he said with a smile

Camryn stepped to the side so that they could enter and Phoenix was in awe of her best friend's new place. She, like Camryn, immediately fell in love with the high vaulted ceilings. Giving them a tour of her new home, Camryn walked in and out of rooms breathing heavily.

They stopped in the room that Camryn had decided she would make the nursery.

"Look at that belly," Phoenix smiled, rubbing Camryn's small, round tummy. Words couldn't express how ecstatic she was that her best friend would soon be someone's mother.

"I can't believe I'm about to have a damn baby," she smiled, looking downwards.

"Babe, can we have a minute?" Phoenix asked as Jy stepped back and headed back down the stairs.

"He seems like a good guy," Camryn said as she looked out of the window. Phoenix stood on the opposite side, looking out as well.

"He really is, Cam. He's so calm and he lets me be me, without judging me or anything. That's all I ever wanted. Bitch, we haven't talked in a minute. How about my no good ass husband popped up at my mom's house begging for another chance and I curved his ass."

"What?! Are you serious?" Camryn asked. Phoenix's news kind of stunned her. She knew how desperate Frederick was for her to sign the divorce papers. It was almost as if he couldn't wait to get rid of Phoenix, so she was surprised that he had gone to her mom's house.

"Dead ass serious. Jy pulled up and Frederick tried to get hype with his scary ass. You should have seen how his bitch ass was carrying on. Ain't no way in hell I would take him back after he made a whole family on my ass." Phoenix found herself getting upset just thinking about it. She knew that had she not been with Jy, a chance would have possibly persisted and that's what she hated.

"Fred needs to sit his ass down some damn where. He made his dam bed and now he needs to lay in it. Fuck him, boo! Jy seems like a good guy, so appreciate that shit because they damn sure don't exist," Camryn said before walking away from the window. Phoenix saw Camryn getting emotional so she walked behind her dear friend to console her.

"You haven't told him yet, have you?" she asked, causing Camryn to stop walking. Camryn turned to face her best friend with a face full of tears. She shook her head no because she was ashamed. She knew that the way she was doing Syd was wrong, but it felt like the right thing to do. She missed him more than she would allow herself to admit. "Ah hell nah Cam, that shit ain't cool. How can you not tell that nigga that you're about to have his baby? He deserves to know, boo. If nothing else, he deserves that much. I understand the relationship is over, but damn, give him the chance to be a father. He's already a great father to his son, right?"

Camryn nodded her head. She couldn't deny that Syd was a great father to his little boy with Ursula. She knew he would be a great dad to their child also, but didn't want the drama that would follow him.

"He is, and I know I fucked up, but I have been at peace so far during this pregnancy. True enough, a bitch be lonely as hell but I am at peace. I started brand new and I'm loving every second of it. I won't sit here and lie and say I don't miss him, because I do and that's what hurts the most."

"You damn sure did start brand new; bitch got a new car and all," Phoenix laughed while Camryn rolled her eyes.

"Bitch, who trades in a BMW for a Hyundai? You got me fucked up! That shit is a rental. That dumb bitch Vicious keyed my damn car, so it's in the shop," Camryn spat. Phoenix's blood boiled at the mention of Vicious' name.

"When did you see that bitch?"

"Girl, that bitch followed me to the gas station. I saw her at the wing place and she flashed that ol' fake smile at me, but I was like fuck her. I left the place and stopped at the gas station. While on my way out the store, she was keying my fuckin' car," Camryn said.

"You lie!" Phoenix couldn't believe Vicious would be that brazen to do such a thing in broad daylight.

"No, I'm not. Lemme show you," Camryn said as she pulled out her phone and pulled up the pictures. "Look." She handed the phone to Phoenix and she gawked at the pictures.

"What did you do? I mean, I know if you weren't pregnant, you would have fucked her up. But, in your condition, what'd you do?"

"Well, the fact that I was pregnant wasn't going to stop me from giving her what she deserved. I stuck my hand in my purse and pulled out my hot sauce spray…"

"Camryn, you didn't!" Phoenix said with a huge smile on her face.

"I sure did. I tabasco pepper sprayed that ass with a quickness. I bet her ass won't fuck with me ever again in her pitiful fuckin' life. I'm not fighting these hoes anymore, Phoenix; especially not while I'm pregnant. My baby has really made me realize that the bullshit doesn't matter anymore, nor does it need to be addressed. I lost myself working at Club Lush. I became just like the rest of those ratchet bitches and that ain't me. I'm educated and smart and I deserve better than the life I was living."

"My sentiments exactly. Frederick would make my ass go back to jail, because his baby mama is a gutta rat. These hoes mad because they can never be us, that's all. Enough about all that though; you need to tell that man, Camryn. Don't make that baby suffer because of what y'all got going on. It's not fair to him or the baby."

Camryn took heed of everything that Phoenix was saying, but she still didn't know if she was ready. She knew that when the time came, Syd would be pissed and possibly want nothing to do with her. Her heart ached at the thought of him turning his back on her for not telling him sooner.

"I know it and I will tell him. Thanks boo," Camryn said.

"I love you, Cam."

"I love you too."

"Well, let me get on out of here."

They hugged once more as Phoenix turned to leave. Camryn had a lot of decisions to make, but what she didn't know was that she was running out of time.

Chapter Seven

Syd had been waiting in Camryn's driveway for the past three evenings and she never once came home. He wondered what the hell was going on with her. Where the hell had she been spending her fucking nights if she hadn't been coming home? Finally on the fourth evening, a car pulled in behind him and popped the trunk. Syd didn't know what the fuck was going on. A black woman got out of the car and headed to the trunk.

She retrieved a hammer and a sign and commenced to hammering the 'FOR SALE' sign in the front yard. Syd immediately jumped out of the car, alarming the woman. She held the hammer up in a defensive mode.

Syd raised his hands and said, "I ain't tryna hurt you, lady. I just wanna know why you have a 'FOR SALE' sign up in front of this house."

"The house is up for sale," she said. "Would you like to see the inside?"

"I already know what the inside looks like."

"Oh okay. Would you like to put in an offer then?" she smiled.

"Hell no! This my ol' lady's house! Where she at?" Syd asked.

"Ummm, if she's your ol' lady, wouldn't you already know where she is?"

"Lady please, I am not in the mood for your smart shit! I've been sitting in this fuckin' driveway for the past three evenings waiting on her. She ain't never come home.

Matter of fact, I ain't seen nobody but you. So, can you please tell me where she is?" he asked.

"I'm sorry. I'm not at liberty to divulge that information. All I can tell you is that she moved and put the house up for sale. Why don't you just call her and ask her?" the woman said.

"Lady please…"

"Please nothing, sir. There is nothing I can do. My hands are absolutely tied." The woman placed the hammer in the trunk of the car and said, "I'm gonna need you to move your car from this property or I will be forced to call the police and tell them you are trespassing."

"Ain't that about a bitch!" Syd said through clenched teeth.

The woman hurriedly slid into the front seat of her car and locked her door. She thought Syd looked like a thug and she wanted no parts of whatever he had on his mind for her. She was not about to be another statistic. She started her car and backed out of the driveway full speed. Syd just shook his head and got in his car. He needed to see Camryn and he needed to do it soon. He had to know if she was pregnant and if she was, why hadn't she told him? She knew how much he loved her, so why would she keep something so important from him?

He didn't have a choice but to take his ass home.

****

Vicious stood in the jail cell, waiting for the other cellmate to finish with the phone. She had been trying to call her mom for the past two days and had been unsuccessful. She couldn't understand why her mom wasn't answering the phone. She needed her to come down to the jail and post her bail. She was tired of being locked up in that hell hole with these filthy ass women. She didn't belong there and felt as if she had worn out her welcome.

At one point, she had even pushed her pride aside and called Hennessy. She had high hopes that her once best friend would answer the phone and rush down here to bail her out. But, she didn't even bother to pick up. Vicious had left her two voicemail messages and she still sat in jail.

She huffed and puffed in an effort to get the girl off the phone faster. Instead of hanging up the phone, the girl said into the phone, "I don't know what this bitch standing here breathing all hard for. I will get off the phone when I'm fuckin' ready to get off the phone."

Vicious stood there and rolled her eyes, because she just knew the bitch on the phone was not getting flip with her. She sucked her teeth and moved away from the girl. She wasn't trying to get in any more trouble than she was already in. The girl finally decided to get off the phone about twenty minutes later. She hung the phone up and moved away from the area. Vicious immediately picked up the phone and began to wipe the ear and mouth piece on her shirt.

"Bitch, what the fuck you doing that for?" the girl asked.

"Ain't nobody trying to catch no disease or infection from you," Vicious responded.

"FUCK YOU, BITCH!" the girl hollered.

"FUCK YOU TOO!" Vicious yelled back.

She was sick and tired of people constantly getting over on her. She still couldn't believe that she was still sitting in jail because she keyed Fendi's car. She had expected to be gone since yesterday, but since her mom hadn't answered the phone, she was still stuck in jail. Her eyes had finally stopped burning from the pepper spray that Fendi had attacked her with. She had no idea that pepper spray burned so much.

She finally dialed her mom's number and she finally picked up on the third ring. She waited for the operator to patch her through and when her mom's voice finally came over the line, she breathed a sigh of relief.

"What the hell have you gotten yourself into now, Vicky?" her mom fumed.

"Mom, what makes you think I did anything wrong?"

"Because your ass is calling me from jail! What the hell did you do?" her mom repeated.

"I just got charged with destruction of property."

"Destruction of property?! So that means you made a conscious decision to fuck up someone's shit. Whose shit did you decide to fuck up and get caught behind?"

"No one, ma. Can you just please come bail me out? My bail is $2500 but if you get a bail bonds…"

"BLAH! BLAH! BLAH!" her mom interrupted. "Don't you think I've been through this shit enough times to know the damn routine?"

"Okay, so you're gonna come get me?" she asked her mom.

"Hell no!"

Her mom was sick and tired of her bullshit. She was tired of bailing her daughter out of jail, only to have her go back and get herself in trouble again. She figured now was a good time to hit her daughter with some tough love. Maybe if she sat in jail for a week or two, she would learn a lesson and grow the hell up. She was tired coughing up her Bingo money to a daughter who didn't appreciate her damn freedom. If she didn't appreciate her freedom before, maybe some more time in jail would help her appreciate it next time she got out.

"What do you mean?" Vicious asked. She was stunned that her mom would just leave her in jail. Her mom had always bailed her out. That was why she didn't give two shits about getting arrested; because she knew once her mom found out, she would rush down to get her.

"I mean, HELL NO! Did I stutter?" her mom asked with an attitude.

"MOM! You can't possibly leave me here!"

"The hell I can't! Every time you get your ass in trouble, I come running to bail you out! For what? For you to go right back in jail again, because you can't stop messing with people. I'm tired of going through the same shit. I'm tired of having to use my good money to get you out of your messes."

"So, you're really not going to come get me?"

"No, I'm not. I have plans for my money, but I bet that never occurred to you because you think whatever money I get should be spent on your bail…"

"Mom, what about all the money I've been giving you over the past years? I've always given you money and a lot of it! Doesn't that count for anything?"

"Yes, after the years I've spent cleaning your ass and bailing you out of jail, I'd say we're even."

"Wow! I can't believe you're going to actually leave me sitting in here."

"I suggest you get comfortable because you will be there until your time is served or unless someone else gets you out. Now, I've got plans so toodle loo," her mom said before ending the call.

"MOM! MOM!" she yelled into the phone. "MOM!"

The girl who had given her trouble with the phone burst into laughter. Vicious eyed the girl with hatred in her eyes. She was sick and tired of the bitch getting in her business. As the girl continued to laugh at Vicious, she stood up and made her way over to where the girl was sitting. She was going to teach that bitch to mind her own fucking business, once and for all.

****

After speaking with the real estate agent about Camryn's house being put up for sale, Syd knew he had to speak with her. He had to find out if what Ursula had told him was true. He needed to know if she was really carrying his baby. So, the next morning, Syd decided if he was going to get any answers from Camryn, he was going to have to do something drastic. He set his alarm to wake him at six in the morning. He got up, stretched, then went into the bathroom to take care of his personal hygiene. He relieved himself before brushing his teeth and washing his face. Once he was done, he hopped in the shower and then got dressed. He was on a mission to find out the truth and he wasn't going to stop until he did.

Syd pulled up to Bartholomew Elementary and parked in the handicapped space directly in front of the school's entrance. He knew for a fact that he wouldn't miss Camryn parked in that spot. As he sat and waited for her to walk by, he rested his head against the headrest and turned up his music. He continuously dozed off, but he knew he couldn't fall asleep.

"Sir, you can't park here," the school's parking lot monitor said as Syd sat up. As he was about to speak, he saw Camryn getting out of her car a few cars down.

"Aight man, take your ass on. I'm about to move," he spat as he tried to focus on what he had come to do. The monitor walked off while talking on his walkie-talkie as Camryn strutted by, throwing her bag over her shoulder. Tears filled Syd's eyes as he stared at her protruding belly. The pain inside of him couldn't be denied. He couldn't believe that she had gone through such great lengths to keep her pregnancy away from him.

Jumping out of his car, Syd looked at his G-Shock and smiled, realizing that students wouldn't start arriving for another thirty minutes. He walked inside of the building and looked down the hall as Camryn entered her classroom. Taking a deep breath, Syd took baby steps towards Camryn's classroom. He tried with all his might to conjure up the words he would say, the actions he would do, the way he would feel. Tears continued to rain down his face as he stood in front of her door. Turning the knob slowly, he walked inside as Camryn jumped back. He wanted to be mad at her ass, but he couldn't; he loved her just that much. He wanted to cuss her out for keeping such an important aspect of his life away from him, but all he really wanted to do was hold her.

Camryn stood in fear. She had managed to hide her pregnancy from Syd for almost five months, but he had finally caught up with her. She wanted to run, but she was tired of running. She wanted to scream, but she was tired of doing that too.

"Why Cam?" Syd asked, wiping the tears from his face. Camryn had managed to break him down emotionally and mentally to the point that he no longer felt like a man.

"Not here ok... please Syd, just leave," she uttered as tears started to well up in her eyes. She felt like shit for causing Syd such great pain. She hadn't been this close to him in months and her heart smiled because she missed him something terrible.

"BITCH AIN'T NO..." Syd found himself getting angry as he stepped back and inhaled. He never wanted to call her out her name. He loved her so much and looking at her, pregnant with his seed overwhelmed him. He couldn't understand how she could have kept this from him. "Camryn, this shit ain't cool, ma. How could you keep something like this from me? I feel like a fool, yo! You got my baby mama laughing at my ass and calling a nigga a deadbeat when I didn't even know shit about you carrying my seed. That shit hurts. That was selfish as fuck. Why would you do that to me? And I know you didn't plan on me finding out because your trifling ass done moved without giving me a forwarding address!" he spat.

"I'm sorry, Syd. I planned on telling you about the baby, but I couldn't bring myself to do it. I saw each time you came to my house and it killed me to not give in, because I yearned for you. The reason I didn't tell you is because every time we try to make this thing work, we end up with nothing but drama. I'll admit that I was wrong for keeping this baby from you, but I thought I was doing the right thing. I don't want..."

"The right thing?! How the fuck is this right, ma? Right for who? You had no intention on telling me shit because the fact still remains that you moved and didn't tell me where you were. You planned on taking my baby and getting the fuck on." Syd was livid. He noticed the way each time he inched closer to Camryn, she shifted to protect something on her desk. He noticed a packet of papers on her desk, which caused him to snatch them. His eyes darted back and forth between Camryn and the papers.

"Transfer papers, huh? I can't believe this shit. I have a kid on the way and the bitch I would move mountains for didn't even give a nigga a heads up." Syd rubbed his temples, trying to calm himself down. He knew he had called Camryn out her name again, but this time, he meant it.

"I know you're mad and all that and I know I fucked up, but I won't be too many more bitches. I didn't disrespect you, so let the respect be reciprocated," Camryn spat, taking a seat behind her desk. Syd looked at her as if she had two heads.

"Respect? Why do you feel you deserve that? I've never been a deadbeat nigga and I would never let a woman treat me as such. You want me to respect you after you did something like that to me? Same ol' Camryn, thinks the world revolves around her ass. I'll admit, I did some shit to you that I shouldn't have done, but I didn't deserve this Cam. You shot me and my dumb ass still wanted to be with you. Niggas were knocking at your door left and right when I was staying at your crib, but I looked pass that shit because I loved the fuck out of you. Hell, I still do, so don't kick shit like I was the only one fucking up. It don't matter what we went through, I should have known about my kid."

Camryn sat with her head down, trying to hide the tears that fell at a rapid pace. Syd was right about everything he had said, but her pride wouldn't allow her to admit that she was wrong. He was the reason she had kept this baby in the first place. She wanted a piece of him, no matter what happened in the end.

****

"Shit, right there, baby! Don't stop!" Phoenix pleaded as Jyri used his tongue to dance with her kitty-kat.

"Right there?" he asked as he nibbled gently on her clit. Phoenix gyrated her hips meeting Jy's tongue halfway. Her juices saturated his tongue. Jy stood from the edge of the bed and wiped Phoenix's juices from his beard as he removed his Balmain jeans. Taking off his boxers, Jy stroked his eight inch member slowly. Phoenix's mouth salivated at the sight of his perfect mushroom head. Jy rolled a rubber down his shaft and positioned himself in between Phoenix's legs. Entering her slowly, Phoenix wrapped her legs around his waist and pulled him in with force. She couldn't remember the last time she had sex, so she had no time to play. Her pussy throbbed each and every time they were together and she had been anticipating this moment.

"Shit, this muhfucka wet as fuck," Jy admitted as he buried his head in the crooks of Phoenix's neck. Each thrust he delivered, she matched with pride. Jy plunged in and out of her, hitting her deepest spots.

"I'M ABOUT TO CUMMMM!" Phoenix yelled as her legs started to shake. Jy pushed her legs back to the point that her toes were against the headboard, as he went deep down feeling the effects of her orgasm exploding.

"FUCKKKK!" Jy yelled as he shot his kids into the condom. Neither Phoenix nor Jy had any energy left as they rolled over, trying to catch their breaths.

"That shit was lit ma," he confessed, causing her to blush.

She knew the damage she had between her legs, but to hear him say it was a plus. Phoenix got up and went into the bathroom. Turning on the water, she lathered a rag and commenced to washing herself up. Once she was done, she grabbed another and went back into the bedroom to wipe Jy down.

"You hungry?" he asked.

"Hell yeah! We can get something quick for now. I was thinking about doing a seafood boil tonight, what you think? I can invite Cam over and you can invite some of your homeboys."

"Sounds like a plan."

Phoenix threw on a pair of PINK leggings with a PINK tank top, some flip flops to match and she headed to the grocery store. She knew Camryn was still at work, but she had texted her and said that she would come. Jy had already left and said that he would be back later, so she decided to stop and grab a bite to eat from McDonald's. Any other day, McDonald's wouldn't have gotten a dime of her money, but she was hungry and needed something right then.

As Phoenix pulled around, she fumbled through her Gucci handbag for her wallet. Looking down, Phoenix grabbed a twenty from her wallet and proceeded to hand the cashier her money. When she saw Brazailia standing behind the register, she burst into a fit of laughter.

"Girl, I know your overgrown, smart mouth ass ain't minimum wagin' it out at Mickey D's. I know you didn't let that nigga play you like that," she continued, slapping her hand against her thigh as she laughed out loud. Brazailia's nostrils flared in anger. The last person she expected to see was Fred's wife. She couldn't believe that Phoenix was standing here clowning her.

A couple of weeks ago, Fredrick had sent her back home. When she got there, she was shocked to find that someone had cleaned out her house. So, she was forced to come back out here, but Fred was adamant about their relationship being over. To add insult to injury, he wouldn't give her any extra money unless it concerned their kids.

"Thank you come again," Brazailia spat as she slammed the window in Phoenix's face. She needed this job and she wasn't about to let her baby daddy's ex-wife make her feel any less of a woman than she already felt. Phoenix pulled off and grabbed her food from the second window, while Brazailia stood back and watched. She was jealous of Phoenix because she was beautiful and she knew that Fredrick still loved her. It didn't make it any better that her body was to die for.

"Is everything ok? That woman said we should check on you because you were hot and bothered?" Brazailia's manager questioned. She wanted so badly to run out, but getting emotional and breaking down wouldn't pay her bills.

"I'm fine," she spat as she rushed towards the back. There was no way in hell she would allow anyone to see her being weak. True enough, she worked at McDonald's, but she was doing what she had to do to survive and take care of her kids. She didn't know how it came to this. When she met Fred in his military uniform, she saw things going a totally different way. How did she end up a single parent with not one, but two kids?

If only she could turn back the hands of time…

****

"Jy, would you get the door, babe? That might be Cam," Phoenix yelled from upstairs as she got dressed. She had prepared crab legs, shrimp, corn on the cob, baby red potatoes, and smoked sausages and she couldn't wait to dig in. Jy had mentioned that three of his homeboys were coming over and she felt a bit nervous, being that she and Camryn would be the only females. She looked in the mirror and admired her small toned frame. Her red and white sundress fit a little snug, but she was feeling lovely.

Making her way downstairs, Phoenix looked at her best friend and Jy engaging in a conversation and smiled. It warmed her heart to see Jy opening up to Camryn when

Fredrick had never done as much. The doorbell rang and Jy went to answer it as she made her way over to Camryn. As she sipped her cranberry juice, Jy's guests walked in. Camryn spit out her juice as she locked eyes with Syd.

The two of them stared at each other for an awkward moment. They hadn't spoken since Syd had shown up at the school a couple of days ago. Jy looked at the two of them and asked, "You two know each other?"

"Yea, this the woman I told you about… the one that was trying to hide her pregnancy from me," Syd said as he continued to stare at Camryn.

Her face took on a flushed look as she blushed with embarrassment. She couldn't believe Syd had just put her business on front street like that in front of strangers. She didn't care that he said it in front of Phoenix, because she already knew everything about what had been going on between the two of them. She didn't know Jy that well and didn't appreciate that Syd had not only blasted her in front of him, but in front of Phoenix's other guests.

Camryn was livid and wanted to leave right then and there, but she wasn't about to let Syd ruin her night with her best friend. She could see that Jy was surprised to find out that she was the woman that Syd had apparently been talking about. She wasn't sure exactly what Syd had told him, but she was sure that he mentioned her pregnancy and how she hadn't told him about it.

Instead of responding, she turned on her heels and headed to the kitchen. Phoenix quickly followed behind her. Camryn stood with her arms against the countertop as she tried to catch her breath. Phoenix came up behind her and asked, "Are you okay?"

"Yea, I'll be fine. I was just surprised to see him, that's all."

"Is everything alright?" Jyri asked.

"Yea babe, everything is fine," Phoenix said.

DING DONG! DING DONG!

"I'll get the door." Jyri left the kitchen to go answer the door. What surprised the shit out of him was when he pulled the door back and Hennessy stood on the other side. He was not expecting her to show up here. He immediately pushed her out the door and grabbed her by her arm, trying to get her to her car.

"What the fuck are you doing here?" he asked through clenched teeth.

"I knew that was your fuckin' car! The question is what are you doing here?!" Hennessy was pissed. She knew that Lambo belonged to Jyri, because no one else had one like it in the city. She was passing by and saw the car parked outside and knew it was Phoenix's house. She wondered what the hell he was doing there, so she stopped to find out.

"Why are you here? You need to leave!"

"Is this why you broke up with me? Is this why you wanted me to have an abortion? Because you were messing with that bitch!" she yelled.

"Keep your fuckin' voice down before the neighbors hear you!" he hissed.

"That ain't why you want me to keep my voice down. You want me to be quiet so that bitch doesn't hear me! Well, guess what? I don't give a fuck who hears me!" she yelled.

"Get the fuck out of here!" he said as he continued trying to get her to get in her car.

All of a sudden, the front door opened and everyone filed outside. Phoenix looked at Camryn and they were both speechless that Hennessy had showed up at her house. Why was she here and how the hell did Jy know her?

Phoenix approached and placed her hand on her hip. "What the hell is going on here? Why the fuck are you here, bitch?" Phoenix asked.

"She was just leaving," Jyri stated.

"How do you even know her?" Phoenix asked as she stood with her arms across her chest.

"Yea Jy, tell them how you know me," Hennessy said as she placed her hand on her hip.

"Are you cheating on me… with that… that… that troll?!" Phoenix asked angrily.

"Troll? Bitch, I will…"

WHAP!!

Before Hennessy could say another word, Phoenix had reached around and popped her in the mouth. "Oh no, bitch!" Hennessy said as she got ready to fight. Jy held her and opened her car door.

"Go home! Get the hell out of here!" he said.

"That bitch just punched me and you want me to go home?! Hell no!" Hennessy said.

"Get the fuck out of my damn yard, bitch!" Phoenix yelled.

"You made me get an abortion for that bitch! You are unbelievable!" Hennessy said as tears sprang to her eyes.

"ABORTION!!" Camryn and Phoenix hollered.

"Yea, I was pregnant with our kid six months ago and he begged me to get an abortion because he wasn't ready. If I had known he was playing house with your bitch ass, I would have kept my baby. But, I had the abortion because I thought it would bring us closer," Hennessy confessed.

"And how did that work out for you, bitch?!" Phoenix asked with a smirk on her face. She was pissed to the max.

"YOU BITCH!" Hennessy yelled as she lunged for Phoenix. Jy caught her and threw her ass in her car.

"Get out of here before you get arrested!" he told her.

"You are unbelievable!"

"Shit between us have been over for a long time now! Just leave me alone and go about your business!" he said to a crying Hennessy.

"You'll regret this! All of you will regret this shit!" she said as she finally started her car and backed out of the driveway. She peeled off down the road, leaving the smell of burned rubber in her wake.

Everyone turned to go back inside the house. Phoenix and Jy stayed outside, because she needed to get shit cleared up ASAP.

"What the hell was that about? Are you cheating on me, Jy?" Phoenix asked.

"Hell no! I dated that girl a year ago, but we broke up eight months ago. Six months ago, she came to me and told me that she was pregnant and that the baby was mine. Because we weren't a couple anymore and I didn't want to be tied to her for the rest of my life, I told her to get rid of it. The only reason she said she would was if we got back together. I told her what I needed to tell her so she would have the abortion, but I never intended to get back with her. She just had too many damn insecurities!" he explained.

Phoenix listened to him and the sincerity in his voice let her know that he was telling the truth. But, why didn't he mention her beforehand? When she thought about that question, she realized that she was being unreasonable about the situation. After all, the two of them weren't married, so he had no reason to confess anything about Hennessy to Phoenix.

"I'm sorry that she just showed up here. Please don't let it spoil our day," Jy begged as he pulled Phoenix into his arms.

"I hate that girl. Well, hate is a strong word, but I definitely loathe her."

"How do you even know her? I didn't think the two of you ran in the same circles whatsoever," he commented.

"Well, we don't run in the same circles. I know her because unfortunately, we used to work together," Phoenix confessed.

"Work together? The only thing she's ever done was dance at that weak, triflin' ass club, the Lush or something like that. Wait…" Jy said as he began to put two and two together. "Are you a stripper?" The look on his face was one of confusion. He didn't know that much about Phoenix's past or what she did for a living. He just fell for her hook, line and sinker without even getting very much info on her.

"Oh God, please don't tell me that you shed your clothes at that club!" he said.

Chapter Eight

Drew and his wife had been having trouble getting along ever since Camryn had outed him. He never thought that she would tell his wife the truth about him and Tucker. Even though she did keep the name of his male lover out of the conversation, she still let his wife know that he was dipping in the muddy holes of the same sex. He had high hopes that she would just run with the excuse he had given his wife about her being the reason he rented those hotel rooms. But, since she hadn't cosigned, shit in his marriage was all fucked up.

"I want you out of this house!" his wife repeated the words she had consistently been saying for the past two weeks since she found out.

"I'm not leaving! We are going to sit down and talk about this and work things out," Drew said.

"Are you fucking kidding me?!"

"Keep your voice down," Drew said through clenched teeth. "You don't want to alarm the children."

"Alarm the children? You don't think they already know that something is wrong between us? You're sleeping in the guest room and we haven't been communicating with each other like we used to. Our children already know that our marriage is fucked up!" she said.

"But... but, we can fix it if you want to."

"I don't want to! I don't want to be in a marriage with a man who is sleeping with other men!"

"I'm not sleeping with other men!" he said.

"So, Miss Peters is lying... is that what you're saying?"

"Y-y-y-yes... she's lying," he stuttered. His wife picked up on the fact that he was lying by the way he stuttered. Hell, every time her husband lied, he stuttered his way through it.

"You're the liar, Drew and I want you out of this house. We are never going to work things out! You're a... a... a faggot!" she cried. She placed her hands over her face and began to cry. She couldn't believe that the man she had been married to for almost twelve years was dipping his dick in the assholes of other men.

How the hell could she live that down? The shit was downright embarrassing and she hated that she had to live in a city when she knew people were talking about her. Her children would have to go to school in shame because their classmates' parents knew about her husband and his gay liaisons. What kind of man would put his family through this shame? What kind of man kept secrets like this from his wife he supposedly loved? How could any man still look his wife in the eyes and tell her that he loved her when he was fucking other men?

Just the thought of how nasty that was made her want to vomit where she stood.

****

Hennessy drove through the streets like a bat out of hell, trying to get away from Phoenix's house. She couldn't believe that Jy had played her to the left the way he had. There was something about the authority in his voice that let her know that he was deep in with Phoenix.

"I'm so tired of those bitches winning," she scoffed, punching the steering wheel. Every which way she turned, Phoenix and Fendi were winning at everything she tried to do. She was tired of Phoenix and didn't know how much more she could take.

"FUCK THIS!" she yelled before busting an illegal U-turn in the middle of the street. Cars honked their horns at her irrational behavior. Hennessy stuck her middle finger out of the window as she made her way back to Phoenix's house. She prayed that she wouldn't get her ass whopped again, because they were known for their hand work. There was no way in hell she would let Phoenix win again when her feelings were so powerful. Swerving into Phoenix's driveway, Hennessy hopped out of her Lexus and slammed the door. Strutting her way to the front door, she proceeded to beat the door as hard as she could.

BOOM! BOOM! BOOM! Banging like the damn police until she got a reaction.

"JY, OPEN THIS GOTDAMN DOOR RIGHT FUCKIN' NOW!" she hissed. Phoenix swung the door open and stared her down menacingly.

"Bitch, what do you want? Can we not enjoy our day for once, without your begging ass bothering us?"

Hennessy looked past Phoenix and nudged her to the side and stormed over to where Jy, Syd, and Rico sat playing a game of Madden 2K17.

"Oh, this bitch has lost her got damn mind. Jy, you better get that ho'!"

Jy turned around as Hennessy stood with her hand on her hip. Fendi looked her up and down, itching to lay hands on her, but in her current condition, she knew she would never hear the end of it if she did.

"Your ass is lucky I can't touch you," Fendi spat with one hand on her hip and the other on her stomach.

"BUT I CAN!" Phoenix fired back as she wrapped her hand around Hennessy's twenty-six inch weave. She proceeded to drag her out her home as Hennessy was swinging wildly, trying her best to touch Phoenix.

"JY, TELL THIS BITCH TO GET HER HANDS OFF OF ME! THIS SOME EXPENSIVE ASS LOCKS SHE GOT HER FUCKIN' HANDS IN!" Hennessy pleaded, while Jy stood back laughing hysterically with the other men.

"Hell nah! I told you to take your dumb ass on, but you wanted to test the waters. Get the fuck on ma, ain't shit here for you," he retorted.

Phoenix pushed Hennessy out of the door and kicked her in the back of the knee, causing her knees to buckle and her to fall face first. Flushed in embarrassment, Hennessy looked at Jy and swung her hair out of her face while tears welled in her eyes.

"I can't believe you're really playing me like this… after everything I did for you. You promised me so much, yet you're taking it away because of this bitch," she shot back, pointing at Phoenix.

"You don't have another time to call me a bitch, ho'! You got some nerve walking in my shit and disrespecting me like I won't beat your ass. Bye Hennessy, go on before I forget that I'm trying to change."

Hennessy got up and limped her way to her car while everyone stood and laughed at her pain. She felt like shit once again as she sped off.

"I'm going to get you Phoenix. I swear I will," she said as if Phoenix was standing in front of her. She headed to her home with revenge on her mind. As she turned into her driveway, her phone started ringing in her cup holder.

"HELLO!" she yelled.

"You have a collect call from an inmate at the Baton Rouge County Jail...Vicious-"

Hennessy removed the phone from her hear and cackled. How amusing was it that Vicious was in the same predicament she was in a while back and was now calling her for help. When she was in that situation, Vicious hadn't done anything but turn her back on her. Itching to laugh at Vicious, Hennessy quickly accepted the call.

"Hennessy?" Vicious hesitantly said. Pain was evident in her voice, causing Hennessy to smile through her own pain.

"Yep, how may I help you?"

"I really need your help. I have been in here for almost a month and I'm losing my sanity. If you come and get me, I promise I will pay you back as soon as I get out."

Hennessy smiled at hearing Vicious damn near begging for assistance.

"I find it funny that we were just in this same predicament not too long ago. Only difference was I was on the receiving end and your Gremlin looking ass told me we weren't even friends and that you wouldn't help me. Why should I be the good guy and bail your fake ass out? You haven't done shit for me except laugh at me when I needed you and proved how disloyal bitches can be."

The line fell silent as Vicious tried to gather her thoughts. She caught amnesia when it came to the shit she had done to Hennessy. All she knew was that she was sick and tired of being stuck in that damn jail. People who had been there for a shorter period than her had bailed out and gone home, yet she still remained. Her mom was on some bullshit and wouldn't help.

"Please Hennessy, I have no one else to call. That bitch Fendi got me in here down bad and my mama won't come get me. I have no money in my commissary or anything. If you do this one thing for me, I promise I'll repay you."

Hennessy sat back in her seat with an 'I don't give a fuck' expression plastered on her face. She had been put through the wringer today, so there was no way she was going to allow that bitch to catch her slipping.

"Well, mission failed calling me, bitch because I'm not coming neither. Sit your ass in there and rot, BITCH!" she snapped before ending the call.

****

"That bitch got horse balls bringing her ass up in my house like I don't deliver good ass whoopins'." Phoenix hissed as she downed a glass of cold water. Her blood boiled profusely, thinking of the stunt Hennessy had just pulled. She was at her wits' end with Hennessy and Vicious and wished they would just disappear.

"My bad ma, I didn't mean to bring that drama to your crib," Jy apologized again, but his voice caused Phoenix to become angrier.

"I bet you are... don't you know I will kill you and that bitch? I did this bullshit with my husband and I won't do it again," she snapped. Her eyes sat low as she cut them, shooting darts at Jy.

"AYE, HOLD THE FUCK UP MA! I JUST WENT THROUGH THE SAME 'BULLSHIT WITH THAT SAME HUSBAND YOU'RE REFERRING TO, REMEMBER? NOT TO MENTION THE BULLSHIT AT THE RESTAURANT WITH YOU AND HIS SIDE BITCH! DON'T ACT LIKE YOUR END BEEN A-1! IF IT'S LIKE THAT MA, WE EVEN!" Jy fired back as the veins pulsated in his neck and forehead. He wasn't a lame nigga, so allowing Phoenix to belittle him as if he wasn't one hundred wasn't about to happen. He wasn't the one for the disrespect.

"OH NIGGA, PLEASE! I don't deal with drama, especially when it comes to bitches like Hennessy. You bringing up my ex-husband like this situation is supposed to be overlooked because of a small scuffle. The difference is my ex-husband didn't come to your shit, he came to mines. Hennessy came to my house looking for you and that's what pisses me off."

Phoenix's finger was now in Jy's face while her neck rolled as she tried to get her point across.

"Ok calm down. She is gone, so let's forget about her and enjoy the rest of our day. Y'all airing out each other's dirty laundry when it's nobody's business but your own. At least be grown about it, unlike my baby daddy," Fendi spat, cutting her eyes at Syd.

"Yo, leave me the fuck out of that shit! Don't you even mention being grown about nothing, when you're the same bitch that hid your pregnancy! Or the fact that I had to play bounty hunter to find your dumb ass. Don't fuck with me Camryn… I'm warning you," Syd said, standing up from the couch. Camryn smacked her teeth and rolled her eyes.

"I'll knock them big muhfuggas out their sockets."

"Whatever nigga. Maybe I wouldn't have hid my pregnancy had you not been cheating all the damn time and having my ass out here knocking bitches off their feet."

Camryn stormed off and went to Phoenix's guest room, slamming the door so hard that Phoenix's picture fell off the wall.

"Nah, fuck this! She done pissed me off and I wasn't even done talking to her dumb ass." Syd rushed behind her as his heart smiled. He missed Camryn so much that he didn't mind arguing with her. He walked into the room and closed the door behind him. Camryn sat on the bed in Indian style, bawling her eyes out. All of the feelings she held for Syd came rushing back, but she wanted so badly to get away from him. Syd walked over to Camryn and gazed into her eyes while his hands rested on each side of her stomach.

"We have to stop this shit, ma. I know you miss a nigga because I've been missing you, too. I can't sleep right knowing we ain't together. You're carrying my seed and I don't want us raising my baby in separate homes. I forgive you for keeping my lil one away from me. All I want is for us to work this shit out before the baby comes. Please Cam," he begged.

Syd held her face and kissed Camryn as his heart jumped a beat when she didn't resist. He slipped his tongue into her mouth and their tongues started to dance. Syd snatched Camryn's shirt open exposing her sexy, darkened areolas. Bending down slightly, he slipped her nipple into his mouth while slipping his finger into her moist center. His member was now fully erect as he anticipated the moment he would enter Camryn. He longed for this moment and now that it was here, he wanted to take it slow and gently care for her every need.

"WHAT THE FUCK?" he jumped back, wiping his mouth.

"What?!" Camryn asked in surprise.

"The fuck was that shit in yo titty, ma?" he asked, a disgusted look gracing his handsome face.

"Boy, it was just milk. Now, if you don't come here and give me that dick," Camryn demanded while pulling on Syd's pants. Her mouth salivated at the sight of his caramel colored rod. She adored Syd's flawless mushroom head. It was perfect in every sense of the word. As bad as she wanted to taste Syd, her kitty was throbbing in anticipation of feeling him inside of her. Syd backed Camryn against the bed and she fell back.

"Aye man, be careful with my baby," he said, touching her stomach.

Syd continued to pull Camryn's pants down and rubbed his hand up and down her opening. He stared as Camryn's body and was mesmerized at how beautiful she was. Lying beside her on his back, he nudged her to get on top. Camryn wasted no time hopping on top and sliding down on his rod. It had been over four months since they last had sex so her kitty was super tight. Camryn gasped as Syd's member went deeper inside of her. Biting on her bottom lip, she proceeded to rock back and forth as they moaned simultaneously.

"Fuck bae," he hissed, gripping her hips. "I missed the fuck out of this pussy."

Camryn placed her hand on his chest as she felt her stomach tightening.

"Ah, I'm about to cum babe."

They came in unison as she breathed heavily to catch her breath.

As they caught their breaths, they heard footsteps walking towards the door.

"Y'all nasty asses better take my sheets home and wash them," Phoenix spat from the other side of the door. Camryn buried her head into Syd's neck, filled with embarrassment.

She might have been embarrassed, but that didn't take away from her happiness. She was so excited that she and Syd had reconciled, not only because she loved and missed him, but so they could be a family for their baby. She had wanted them to be a happy family and now they would be.

"I love you, ma," Syd said.

"I love you too." Camryn leaned into him and pressed her lips against his.

Chapter Nine

Vicious sat with her head back in her cell, furious at how Hennessy had treated her. True enough, she knew that she had done Hennessy the same way, but a part of her had hoped that Hennessy would have looked past that. She had been sitting in that cell for an entire month and didn't know when she would be let out. As she sat on the bench with her back against the wall, she wanted to cry. But, as she looked at her surroundings, she knew that wasn't an option. She was in jail so there was no way she was going to show any signs of weakness while she was locked up in here.

"Don't I know you?" a woman with dirty blonde hair and black roots asked as she stared at Vicious.

Vicious looked at the woman and didn't recognize her, so she sneered and responded, "No!"

"You ain't gotta snap at me, bitch! You just look familiar to me."

"Well, I don't know you so if I don't know you, then you don't know me!" Vicious said.

"Well damn. Fuck you too then!" the woman said.

"FUCK YOU, BITCH!" Vicious yelled.

"Keep it down! I got the worse fuckin' headache and don't need to hear all that bull crap from y'all!" some lady that was lying on another bench said.

Vicious didn't want any trouble, so instead of responding, she just rolled her eyes. Three more hours passed and then one of the correction's officers walked up to the cell.

"Rhianna Wright!" she called as she unlocked the cell door.

Vicious jumped up and took off running to the unlocked door. "That's me," she said.

"You've been bonded out!" the officer said.

"WHAT?!" Vicious didn't even wait for the officer to repeat the words. She just ran out of the cell, giddy with happiness. She had been taking showers at the jail and longed to relax in a hot bath filled with bubbles in her own tub. She missed her house. She missed her car. She missed her life.

As much as she hated Fendi and Phoenix, she didn't think she would ever fuck with them again. She never wanted to be back in jail again. She hated the fact that she had to spend so much time in jail and it helped her to realize that she really had no friends. She thought maybe it was time to turn her life around. She needed to change her stage name from Vicious to something else; maybe something sweet and edible.

She just couldn't understand how she had become the person that she was. She didn't want to be that person no more. As she walked out and signed her release papers and collected her property, she saw her mom waiting on the other side of the glass door. She was surprised that her mom was the one to bail her out. She wanted to smile because she was getting released. She was happy that she was finally getting out, but she was pissed that her mom had taken so long to come and get her.

"You have a court appearance on the 13th of next month. You need to be at the courthouse in room 419 by no later than 8:30 that morning. If you fail to appear, the judge will issue a bench warrant for your arrest and you will have to return to jail. Sign here and here," the woman stated.

Vicious signed where she was asked and got the paperwork from the officer. She gathered her belongings and waited for the buzzer to sound so she could exit the area. She walked over to her mom, who was smiling and she couldn't understand why.

"Well damn, the least you can do is smile. I know I'm a lil late, but at least yo ass is out!"

Her mom had no qualms about not coming when she was first called. She had shit to do and was sick and tired of her daughter always getting herself in all kinds of trouble. She felt that it was time for her child to just grow the hell up. She didn't care how Rhianna felt about that. If she would keep her damn nose cleaned, none of that shit would be happening. She was just tired of the bullshit.

Every single time her daughter had ever gotten locked up, she had always spoken to her about making better choices with her life. Yet, no matter how much she spoke to Rhianna, she continued to do her and act as though she were invincible. She was just sick and tired.

"Mom, you left me sitting in this jail cell for a month! A whole freakin' month!" Vicious fumed.

"You lucky I didn't leave you there for another whole freakin' month with the way you talkin' to me! I knew I should have listened to my first damn mind and left you there! That's a nigga for you though… ungrateful ass! I should make you catch the fuckin' bus to your damn house!" her mom retorted.

"I'm sorry mom. I shouldn't have snapped, but do you know how hard that was for me to be stuck in jail all this time?"

"And whose fault is that? Ain't nobody told you to do the crazy shit you be doing! You keyed that woman's car for what? Why would you do some bullshit like that anyway?! You're just out of control and too damn old to be doing childish shit like that!" her mom continued.

"Mom, you don't understand what those bitches put me through…" Vicious tried to defend her actions.

"I don't give a damn what they put you through! It's time for you to grow the hell up and stop blaming everybody because your ass is out of control! You better get yo shit together, because if you don't, next time you get locked up might be yo last. People ain't got time to keep playing these damn games witchu! You too damn grown for that shit!"

"Thanks for bailing me out. I'll change my ways," Vicious said.

"I'll believe it when I see it!" her mom spat.

"Seriously mom… those 32 days I spent in jail were eye openers and that is something I never want to relive again. I ain't never felt so alone. I ain't never felt so useless. I ain't never felt so horrible in my life," Vicious said.

"You stink too," her mom said as she scrunched up her nose.

"Well, I ain't had a bath in 32 days!"

"So, they ain't let you wash ya ass?"

"I washed my ass mom, but I took a shower with some old brittle ass soap. Like I said, I never wanna go back there. UGH! I can't wait to go home and soak in a bubble bath!" she told her mom.

"I can't wait either. I wish I had some cables because if I did, I promise you that I would attach your stinky ass to the roof. Ugh! I'ma have to get my car detailed!"

Vicious looked at her mom and wondered where was her compassion for what she had been through. While her mom was out playing Bingo, she had been locked up in a jail cell. Where the hell was her mom's feelings for what she had gone through? She just needed to know why her mom was so evil and why she treated her the way that she did.

Instead of responding, she just took a deep breath, inside and out.

"Sorry mom…"

"It's okay, as long as you know I want my bail money back and to detail my car. Ain't no way you gon get yo cake and eat it too," her mom complained.

"I'm gonna change. After tonight, I'm turning over a new leaf," Vicious said.

"I sure do hope so, because next time you call me from jail, you will stay there. That's a promise that I plan to keep… no matter what," her mom stated.

"There won't be a next time… believe that!" Vicious said as she stared out the window of her mom's car. She watched as they left the jail behind and thanked God that she was finally free.

At one time, she would have wanted revenge on everyone; Fendi, Phoenix, Dollar, and Hennessy. But now, after serving over a month's time in jail, all she wanted to do was forget every last one of those niggas. She was done with the bullshit. It was time for her to do what her mom said for her to do... she was going to grow up.

****

It was well after two in the morning and Phoenix was exhausted from the day's prior events. Once Jy left, she found herself yelling obscenities and bawling her eyes out. She couldn't figure out why she had such bad luck with men when she knew how good of a woman she was. Rolling over in her bed, Phoenix rubbed the empty space and sighed in frustration. She was tired of sleeping alone when she was supposed to have a man by her side. The only thing good that came out of the night before was that her bestie and Syd had reconciled. Phoenix knew all too well what it felt like to be in love with someone you knew you couldn't be with. She didn't want her godchild growing up without a father.

Grabbing her Samsung S8, she rolled onto her back and checked her phone to see if Jy had called or texted. Feeling defeated that he hadn't reached out, she flipped the covers off of her and stood from her bed. She walked towards her bathroom, but stopped once she heard the sound of glass shattering. She quickly darted over towards the window and looked out. Once she didn't see anything, Phoenix went into the bathroom and peed. With her elbows resting on her knees, she stared off thinking that she would never find happiness. Once she was done, she climbed back into bed and forced herself back to sleep.

Morning came quickly as Phoenix forced herself out of bed. Tired was an understatement when it came to the way she was feeling. Climbing out of bed, she proceeded to take care of her hygiene and get her day started. Once she was out of the shower, Phoenix searched her closet for an ensemble for the day. Opting on a washed pair of denim jeans, Phoenix grabbed a white and silver BeBe shit and her silver BeBe sandals. She walked in front of her vanity and sat down.

Brushing her hair down, she gave herself a middle part. She sprayed herself down with Beyonce's *Heat* fragrance before grabbing her Tory Burch handbag. As Phoenix made her way downstairs, she snatched her keys off the ring and headed outside. Nearing the corner, Phoenix's heart stopped as she stared at her Jeep Cherokee, all fucked up and damaged. All of her windows had been busted out and all of her tires were slashed.

"I know damn well," she spat as she scanned the area. Her blood boiled at the sight before her. Fumbling through her purse, Phoenix retrieved her phone and swiftly dialed Jy's number. She knew without a doubt that Hennessy was responsible and she felt that Jy should pay for it since he was the middle man.

"You got your attitude together today?" Jy questioned without bothering to say hello, which ignited a whole different fire inside of her.

"I damn sure don't. I need you to come to my house ASAP. There's some shit you need to see," she hissed, rolling her eyes as if he was standing in front of her.

Jy heard the seriousness in Phoenix's voice and he knew that something was wrong. Luckily, he was already near her house, so it wouldn't take him long to get there.

"I'll be there in five." He ended the call and rubbed his temple. He hoped and prayed that nothing had happened to Phoenix. Jy turned onto Phoenix's street and sped towards her home. Stopping in front of her house, his nostril flared at the sight of Phoenix's truck looking so disheveled.

"Who the fuck did this?" he spat.

"Like you don't know. I have never had no shit like this until your little sadistic ass bitch came over here on her bullshit. You need to call that bitch and tell her that she's paying for all this. If not, I expect you to pay for it." Phoenix looked at Jy in disgust, even though she knew it wasn't his fault. She was furious that Hennessy was so bold as to pull a stunt like that right in front of her damn house.

"Aye, chill with that attitude shit, ma… real shit. I don't know how the fuck you figure I'm supposed to pay for that shit because a bitch is all in her feelings. That ain't got shit to do with me. I'm supposed to do it because I'm your man, not because of what my ex did. Fuck out of here with that shit, Phoenix. Don't come at me sideways like I'm some bitch nigga."

Jy held so much authority in his voice and it turned Phoenix on in the worst way. She knew she was wrong for coming at him the way she had, but she was just that pissed. She wasn't going to allow Hennessy to deter her from her happiness when she had finally found it. Letting her guard down, Phoenix dropped her arms beside her.

"You're right and I'm sorry. I'm just pissed off babe," she confessed as she stuck her head into his chest. Jy wanted to be mad and cut Phoenix off, but he was stuck. He had never felt another woman the way he was feeling Phoenix and it scared him. He hesitantly wrapped his arms around her resting his chin on the top of her head and inhaled the scent of her hair. Lifting his head, he lifted Phoenix's chin and gazed into her eyes.

"How about we go inside and you show me just how sorry you are?" he laughed, even though he was dead serious.

"You so damn nasty. I would babe, but I have a few errands to run. How about you take me and when we get back, I will cook for you and toot this fat ass up," Phoenix flirted as she slapped his chest while he groped her ass. While her ass sat in Jy's big hands, Phoenix made it clap. Jy bit his bottom lip thinking of the moment he would be in his new favorite place, between her legs. The sexual chemistry between Jy and Phoenix was something you couldn't even fathom.

"Aight, let's roll," he said, walking around and hopping into the passenger's seat.

"What the hell you doing?" Phoenix inquired, a little confused.

"I want to see how sexy you look pushing this fast muhfucka. Besides, I always wanted my lady to chauffeur me around." Jy pulled his seatbelt across his body and buckled in while Phoenix got in and did the same. She was a bit apprehensive about driving Jy's Lambo, because of how fast the car moved. Adjusting the seat and mirrors, Phoenix revved the engine and reversed out of the driveway. She chuckled on the inside as she sped through the Baton Rouge streets.

Pulling into the parking lot at Georgia Power, Phoenix grabbed her handbag and stepped out of the car. She knew Jy was watching, so she made it her business to put an extra sway in her hips. She was making sure he had something good to look at.

"Welcome to Slemco Electric, how may I help you?" the clerk greeted.

"I need to pay my light bill," she responded as she removed her wallet from her bag. Phoenix then gave the clerk her address and identification. She stood silent for a moment while the clerk typed in her information.

"Ma'am, the lights are scheduled to be disconnected. It says here that you called this morning and canceled your service." Phoenix huffed in anger. She knew that she hadn't called and did no such thing.

"I didn't call and do-" stopping mid-sentence, Phoenix rolled her eyes. "That bitch Hennessy."

Chapter Ten

"I'm so happy you're back home babe," Camryn said as she laid her head on Syd's chest. Syd had followed her home the night before and the two had been in a make-up sexcapade ever since. She felt complete knowing that Syd was home and everything was back to normal. She had longed for the day they would reconcile, even though she had played so hard and acted as if she didn't miss him. The truth was, she missed Syd so much sometimes, she felt as if she couldn't breathe.

"Well, this ain't really home since you got a new place and all. I mean, it's gonna take some getting used to but me too, ma. I don't want to go through that shit ever again." He kissed her forehead as she smiled. Staring at the ceiling, Syd smiled as he thought of what life would be like with his newborn and Junior. He wanted everything to be perfect, but there was something he needed to discuss with Camryn first.

"Bae, I've been thinking. I think I want to get out of the game and go legit. This go round, I want everything to be perfect; no more secrets, no more lies, just us and the kids. We've been through so much, but we somehow managed to land right back where we should have been all along, with each other. You're not dancing anymore, so I feel it's only right I go out there and find something that I like to do." Syd shifted and pulled Camryn closer. As their skins touched, the baby started going crazy inside of Camryn's stomach. Syd and Camryn grabbed her stomach and fell in awe at what their little one was doing.

"Looks like somebody's happy that daddy is back," Camryn beamed with glee. Syd kissed Camryn's lips while his hand slipped into her moist center. Her kitty was sore, but she wanted to feel him inside of her once again. Camryn rolled on top of Syd as they shared a long, passionate kiss. Guiding his dick into her walls, she slid down and clenched her pussy muscles tightly around Syd's swollen member, causing Syd to gasp. He stared at all of her naked glory and fell deeper in love with her than he ever had been. Extending his arm and placing his hand around her neck gently, he bit his bottom lip.

"Oh yeah, the next time you shoot me, I'm throwing your ass in the Mississippi River." Camryn laughed while Syd's expression didn't change.

"I'm sorry babe," she hissed as she gyrated her hips, enjoying every inch of the man she so deeply loved.

****

Hennessy was smiling at the handiwork she had done to fuck with Phoenix's life. "That bitch was going to wish she had left my man alone," she muttered to herself as she watched Phoenix from a distance. Phoenix had just walked out of her house and saw the damage that Hennessy had done to her car and she was livid. Hennessy laughed at how easily she could get under Phoenix's skin.

She was more than happy to see her so angry. When Phoenix pulled out her phone, she figured it was to file a police report. She knew she had to get away from there before the police showed up. But, instead of the police showing up, Hennessy almost died when she saw Jyri's car pull into the driveway. "What the fuck is he doing here?!" she questioned to herself.

She watched as Jy got out of his car and spoke to Phoenix. It looked as if the two of them were arguing, which caused an evil smile to spread across her face. She was happy that they were arguing, because in her eyes, that meant they would be breaking up soon. But, when Phoenix rested her head against Jy's chest and he wrapped his arms around her that angered Hennessy more.

She immediately pulled out her phone and looked up the number to the electric company.

"Welcome to Georgia Power Company, how may I help you?" answered the customer service rep.

"I need to disconnect my services please," Hennessy stated.

"Are you relocating? Would you like to transfer your service instead?" she asked.

"Lady, I said I want to disconnect. I didn't say shit about disconnect and reconnect somewhere else!" Hennessy stated angrily.

"What's the service address?" the lady asked.

Hennessy gave her the address and answered a couple of more questions. Thankfully, the woman didn't ask for the last four digits of Hennessy's social security number. She didn't want to have to pull up some bullshit numbers and they wouldn't be able to do what she wanted them to. She had so much attitude with the woman and figured that might be why she didn't ask her. The woman wanted to get rid of her that bad.

"Okay, someone will be out to disconnect services for you no later than tomorrow."

"If you don't send someone out today, you must be paying for services after today," Hennessy said.

"I'll put the order in today ma'am, but I can't make any promises."

Hennessy was so mad, she just hung up the phone. "That bitch was going to stop fucking with me and my good nerves," she said to herself.

She watched as Jy got in the passenger's seat while Phoenix got in the driver's seat. "What the fuck?! He ain't never let me drive his fucking car! What is so special about that bitch that she gets everything she wants? When am I gonna get my fucking turn?!" she wondered out loud.

She started her car and peeled out from the street where she was parked and watching once Phoenix got on the road. She couldn't believe that her life had spiraled out of control that way. How could shit be so fucked up in her life? She had lost her job at the strip club. She had aborted her child. And now, she had lost the man she had killed her baby for. Why was God punishing her this way?

Tears streamed down her face as she raced down the street. She couldn't believe the hands she had been dealt in life. She was entitled to have a happy life just like Fendi and Phoenix. She didn't understand what made them so special that they got to be happy and she couldn't.

She wanted Jyri... she had always wanted him. The two of them had issues, as any couple did, but that didn't mean she didn't want him. She loved that man and thought one day they would get back together. How the hell did Phoenix manage to stick her claws into a man that didn't belong to her? "Jyri is mine! He is the one thing in this world that belongs to me and I'll be damn if that bitch is going to take him from me. She will get hers and wish that she had never fucked with me!"

On her way home, she stopped by the hardware store and purchased a few things that she needed. It was time to wake Phoenix up and let her know that she just couldn't walk over people the way that she had. She couldn't stand Phoenix and wished she had never moved here from wherever the fuck she came from. Her life wasn't the best before Phoenix moved here, but it was better than it is now. She couldn't wait until Phoenix got hers. She was going to enjoy dishing out that shit to that bitch that ruined her life.

****

Mrs. Richardson sat at her post in the front office and smiled at the drama that was taking place in Principal Drew's office. She knew that he had been having sex with Coach Tucker but didn't know that his wife knew. This morning, Principal Drew had just been served with divorce papers and he was livid. His booming voice could be heard from outside the office door as he spoke to his wife.

"How dare you serve me with divorce papers at my job! Do you know how embarrassing that shit is?" Drew spoke to his wife over the phone.

"Well, I certainly wasn't going to have you served here, in front of the children!" his wife shrieked.

"We could have spoken about this when I got home!"

"I'm tired of talking and I'm tired of waiting for you to get the fuck out of my home!"

"OUR HOME!" he yelled.

"MY HOME! I'm the one who has custody of the kids, so I'm going to reside in the home. I don't know where the fuck you are going to go, but if you come back here, I will call the police and have you arrested for trespassing!" she yelled into the phone.

"Tonya that is my house! I am not leaving my house!"

"I bet you will! I changed the locks already and you aren't welcome here anymore!"

"THAT'S MY FUCKIN' HOUSE! You can't keep me out of a house I am making mortgage payments on!" Drew yelled.

"Drew, if you bring your slimy, dirty, busted ass over here, I will shoot you before you make it to the porch! Am I making myself clear?" his wife, Jessica asked.

"You can't..."

"I DID! Now, you can take your dirty ass back to the man whose dick you been twerking on at the motel! We are done!" she said before she ended the call.

"FUUUUUCCCKKKK!!" he yelled as he tossed the phone across the room.

Mrs. Richardson sat behind her desk, a slight chuckle escaped from between her lips. She knew that something like that was going to happen. She wondered what was going on with Tucker and his wife. She hadn't heard anything about their marriage busting up. Maybe, his wife didn't know he was fucking Drew. Wouldn't that be something if a little anonymous bird sent her a note about her husband's muddy dick? She chuckled again at the thought of her little devious mind working.

Mrs. Richardson was old school and a Christian. She didn't believe in all that gay and homosexual stuff. So, in her mind that shit was wrong and God didn't like it. Tucker was deceiving his lil wife who she thought was really nice and could do better. She didn't think it was fair that Drew's marriage was suffering so much and Tucker was still allowed to remain happy in his.

"Humph! Maybe it was time for a little birdie to whisper in Denise's ear and let her know what her husband has been up to behind her back," Mrs. Richardson said to herself. "It's time for the cat to be let out of the bag."

She looked up and said, "Lord, I know you don't want me stirring up trouble, but that little woman is too good to be left in the dark. I know that I will be frowned down upon by you, but I'm sure it'll only be for a little while. She deserves better than him, so I know all will be forgiven when you realize what the big picture is. At least, that is what I pray." She made her sign of the cross, then kissed her fingers before picking up the phone to call the flower shop.

"Jamie's Flower Shop, how can I help you?"

"I need to place an order, but I need my information to remain anonymous. Can you do that?" Mrs. Richardson asked the person on the other end of the phone.

"Yes, we can do that. I'm assuming you want this delivered."

"Yes… to Denise Martin."

"What would you like?"

"A bouquet of roses and the message should read… Roses are red, violets are blue. Check your hubby's dick because it's full of poo-poo. It's time you know the truth. Your husband has been having an affair, but with a man," Mrs. Richardson smiled.

"Oh my!" the woman on the other end commented. "Are you sure you want to send this bouquet out like that? I mean, with that kind of message."

"Yes. Send the bouquet to this address…" she proceeded to rattle off the address and said, "Charge it to this card." She gave her card numbers before saying, "Now, you promised me this would remain anonymous and I expect it to stay that way."

"Yes ma'am. We'll get that out to you today," the woman said.

"Thanks so much!"

Mrs. Richardson ended the call and couldn't help but let out a sinister laugh. She wished she could be a fly on the wall in Tucker's house when he got home. Lord have mercy!

Chapter Eleven

Denise sat inside of her home sipping on a glass of Pink Moscato while watching an episode of *The Bold & The Beautiful*. Dinner was on and her husband would be home soon. Standing from the leather loveseat, Denise was heading towards the kitchen when her doorbell rang.

"Who the hell could that be?" she asked herself out loud. Taking a glance out of the window, she beamed as her eyes landed on a white van with the words *Jamie's Flower Shop* written on the side. Denise was amazed at her husband's gesture and thought that he was full of surprises. Swinging the door open with a huge smile on her face, the delivery guy stood before her, extending his hands to hand over the bouquet. The elegant scent of the mixed roses invaded her nostrils as she lifted them towards her nose and sniffed them. She inhaled their sweet scent and handed the boy a five dollar tip.

"Thank you so much!" she said as she stepped back to close the door. Admiring the roses, Denise sipped from her glass once more before grabbing the card attached. Her eyes weakened at the sight before her. The accusations towards her husband had her stomach in knots. The disgust, the betrayal, and the pain behind the cold words on the card caused vomit to swim around in her stomach. Rushing over to the trash can, her insides came up with force as Tucker ran inside of their home and to his wife's side.

"Denise, what's wrong?" he questioned. Denise used her arm sleeve to clear her mouth of the residue before turning to face him. As hard as she could, she pushed Tucker away from her, causing him to stumble over the barstool. As if that wasn't enough, she started raining blows all over Tucker's head.

"What the fuck is your problem?" Tucker hissed as he tried to block her punches.

With each punch she threw, another tear fell. Her heart weakened at the thought of her husband betraying her, especially with someone of the same sex at that.

"YOU GAY, BOOTY BANDIT MUTHAFUCKA! WHAT THE FUCK IS THIS?!" she snapped, hitting him with the roses. Denise then picked up the card and shoved it in Tucker's face.

Tucker's face twisted into a disapproving scowl as he read what was supposed to be a poem. Whoever had done such an act was trying to ruin his life. Who would be that evil as to play with his marriage and his family? What was that person trying to do to him?

"Listen Niecy, this shit ain't true. It's somebody's idea of a sick joke," he lied. Denise knew her husband was lying, because he called her by her nickname.

"A joke?! A fuckin' joke?! Does it look like I'm laughing, motherfucker?! Nah, that's not a joke someone would play, not with me. GET YOUR SHIT AND GET YOUR GAY ASS OUT OF MY DAMN HOUSE!" she yelled, launching the glass that contained her wine towards Tucker's head. Tucked decided to stand his ground. This was as much his home as it was hers and he wasn't going anywhere.

"I'm not leaving. This is my home too and I have rights. We are going to work this shit out the way married people are supposed to. So, I'm not going anywhere," he spat with his hands interlocked in front of him.

"Like hell you ain't." Denise ascended the stairs and went into the bedroom that they shared. Snatching Tucker's clothes from the hangers, she raised the window and started throwing his shit on the front lawn.

"HE GOT ME FUCKED UP! I DON'T PLAY THAT SHIT! THIS NIGGA WANNA PLAY WITH BOOTY MEAT, LIKE I DON'T DO ENOUGH FOR HIS UNGRATEFUL ASS!" she continued to yell to no one in particular. Tucker barged into their room as Denise threw his shoes into the next door neighbor's pool, one by one.

"WHAT THE HELL ARE YOU DOING?!" He scoffed, playing tug of war with his shoes. Denise bent down and bit Tucker's hand.

"AH, YOU BITCH!" he said before his reflexes kicked in, causing him to backhand Denise. The taste of blood seeped between Denise's teeth.

"You motherfucker," she snapped as she started hitting him simultaneously with his shoe while he begged for her to stop.

"I didn't mean to hit you, I swear." Tucker tried to reach out to Denise, but she slapped his hand away before stomping his big toe. Grabbing her into a bear hug, Tucker fought with Denise as she tried to break free from his grasp.

"LET ME GO AND GET THE HELL OUT OF MY HOUSE!" She pleaded as tears fought for first place down her face.

"I'm not going anywhere and we're going to talk about this. I'm trying to tell you that this shit isn't true. I'm not gay! Now please, you have to calm down so we can work this out."

Just as Tucker let his guard down, Denise brought her knee up into his genitals.

"TAKE THAT TO THAT GAY BASTARD AND SEE WHAT HE CAN DO WITH IT. I WILL FUCK YOU UP IF YOU DON'T GET THE FUCK OUT OF MY DAMN HOUSE!"

Like a thief in the night, Denise walked out of their bedroom, leaving Tucker doubled over wincing in pain.

****

Fredrick sat outside of Phoenix's home, patiently waiting for the moment that she would return. He missed his ex-wife something terrible and he couldn't fathom being away from her another second. Tapping his fingers against his steering wheel, he lifted his Rolex to look at the time. He had been outside of her home for the past three hours and he was becoming irate.

As he started his engine, his face became distorted as he watched Phoenix swerve Jy's Lamborghini into the driveway. Seeing Phoenix smiling so big tore at his heartstrings. He still couldn't believe that she had moved on so quickly, even though their circumstances were so complicated. Fredrick watched as Jy opened the door for Phoenix, allowing her to step out. His blood boiled watching them engage in a passionate kiss. As Jy lifted Phoenix bridal style and proceeded to walk towards the entrance, Fredrick hopped out of his car and stormed their way. He wanted his wife back and he would stop at nothing to get her.

"PHOENIX!" His voice boomed. Jy turned around with Phoenix as she released a frustrated sigh. She was so over Fredrick and his begging ass ways. Jy let Phoenix down and she stared at Fredrick with a grimace on her face.

"What do you want now? We have no ties to one another Fredrick, so can you please just leave me alone?" Fredrick glanced at Jy, then back at Phoenix.

"No I won't. I made mistakes baby and I apologized for those. Please, tell that thug to go home, so that we can discuss this further."

Jy bit the inside of his jaws as his fists rested at his sides. Beyond tired of the way Fredrick continuously disrespected him, he pushed Phoenix behind him and stepped into Fredrick's personal space.

"Look nigga, I don't know you and you sho' as hell don't know me. What I'ma need you to do is turn yo ass back around and go back to wherever the hell you came from," Jy said.

"Look man, I need to talk to MY WIFE and it don't concern you!" Frederick said.

He had military training, so he wasn't afraid of this thuggish nigga. He had been trained to take down the enemies with his bare hands. He was hoping that it wouldn't come to that, but if that was what it took to get his wife to speak to him, then so be it.

"YOUR EX-WIFE!" Phoenix interjected. "We are no longer married Frederick and it doesn't matter how you feel about it. You made mistakes, fine… I forgive you. But, the mistakes you made, you can't take back. I suggest you take your ass back home to your family and forget about me," she said.

"I can't do that."

"Bruh, she asked you nicely to leave…" Jy said, his lack of patience starting to get the best of him.

"This don't concern you, BRUH!" Frederick responded.

Phoenix stepped between the two men and placed her hand on Jy's chest. The last thing she wanted was for her man to get arrested for beating the shit out of Frederick. "Frederick, this is my man! He has been real good to me. He respects me, he treats me like a queen, and he loves me. Why would I ruin what he and I have for something that you and I can't get back? Don't you see… too much has been done. You've hurt me, we've hurt each other. Now, it's time for us to move away from that hurt and just be happy," Phoenix stated.

"I can only be happy with you, baby," Frederick said.

"Well now, we both know that shit ain't true. If it were, we would never have gotten a divorce. You have a girl, a crazy, little project hood rat chick, but she loves you and she's given you two children. Go home Frederick. Go home to her and your kids," Phoenix said.

"But… but… but I love you," Frederick pleaded.

"No, you don't. You just want me because I've moved on. If I were still with you, you would still be running around disrespecting me with other women. Just leave me alone!" Phoenix said.

"Candace please!"

"Look bruh, I've had enough of this shit!" Jy said as he moved Phoenix out of the way. "She told you that she doesn't want yo ass and she never will. You guys are divorced, so I'ma need you to move around some."

"Fuck…"

WHAP!

Before Frederick could get another word out, Jy had punched him square in the jaw. He stumbled back a little but came back swinging. Phoenix stood back and yelled for the two of them to stop. "STOP IT Y'ALL!! PLEASE, STOP THIS!" she yelled.

They were really going at it too. From where she was standing, Jy was whooping Frederick's ass. She didn't want her man fighting her ex, but she was powerless to stop him. Maybe if Jy beat his ass up real good, he would stay away from her. She didn't know how else to get him out of her life. He wanted a divorce, so she signed the papers. The divorce was finalized about five weeks ago. What more did Frederick want from her?

Now that he was free to do what he wanted to do and be with who he wanted to be with, he kept coming back to her. Well, he had better find a way to move on with his life, because no matter how much he came around or begged, she was done.

Her screams finally made Jy stop swinging. He stood up and fixed his dusty clothing as Frederick picked himself up. His nose was bloody and his lip was busted. He also had a cut on his right cheek and a black eye. Yea, her man had done some damage to her ex. She looked at Jy and asked, "Are you okay?"

"I'm straight!" he said as he made his way inside the house, dragging her behind him. He closed the door as Frederick stood there, looking every bit like a lost soul. Frederick didn't know what to do with himself. How could the woman he was once married to just leave him hanging like that?

She didn't even try to check on him or make sure he was alright. She just followed that other nigga in the house and was probably going to go and comfort him and clean him up. Why didn't she just forgive him and take him back so they could get back to the way things used to be? He couldn't understand what her problem was. Was she so hooked on that nigga's dick that she didn't give a fuck about him anymore?

He brushed himself off and got in his car. He backed out of the driveway and headed home. He was so pissed, but his heart was more bruised than anything. He didn't know how much more rejection he could take from the woman he loved.

****

Hennessy left the hardware store and headed home to get ready for a night to remember. She needed to make sure she played her cards right with this. If she did, she would never have to see that bitch Phoenix again and she could have Jy all to herself. She dressed in black sweats, a black shirt, and gloves. She walked over to the bathroom mirror and tied her weave into a ponytail. She slipped her feet into her black Nike Air Max and walked out the door.

She drove in the direction of Phoenix's place with murder on her mind. She thought about the can of paint thinner and the big bottle of lighter fluid and knew that she was about to set the roof on fire. She couldn't wait. She drove the speed limit and took her time. She couldn't afford to get pulled over by the cops. She made sure to follow her speed limit and chanted the song, "The roof... the roof... the roof is on fiyah... we don't need no water, let the muthafucka burn! Burn muthafucka, burn!" She laughed to herself about the evil plot she had conjured up in her head.

She finally pulled on Phoenix's street and crept slowly towards her house. "Aaarrrgghhh!" she screamed when she saw Jy's car parked in the driveway. She looked at the time on the dash and saw that it was almost midnight. Why the hell was he still at her place? Didn't he have his own fucking spot?

She banged her head against the steering wheel. "Dammit! Things never go the way I want them to!" she yelled angrily. Thinking against her better judgment, Hennessy jumped out of her car and popped the trunk. Scanning the area, she made sure no one was outside before she grabbed the paint thinner and lighter fluid from the trunk. Ducking into the neighbor's backyard, she pulled her phone from her pocket and dialed Jy's number... private.

"Yo?" he answered, causing a wicked smile to form across her face.

"Hello sir, this is Promise Hospital of Baton Rouge. I am looking for a Jyri Benton," Hennessy said as she disguised her voice to sound like an innocent nurse.

"This is he."

"Well sir, your mother Belinda Benton has just been brought in and you're listed as her next of kin."

Jyri jumped from the bed, startling Phoenix, who had been lying comfortably in his arms.

"What's wrong, babe?" Phoenix asked in the background, causing Hennessy to roll her eyes. She couldn't stand hearing that bitch's voice. A sinister smile spread across her lips at hearing Jy scuffle to get his things together.

"I'm on the way," he said before ending the call. Hennessy stood on the side of Phoenix's house, behind the bushes as Phoenix's door swung open.

Jealousy engulfed her as she watched Jy and Phoenix run out of the house and to his car. Jy sped out of the driveway and down the street. Taking a deep breath, Hennessy rubbed her hands together and grabbed the products she would use to demolish Phoenix's home. Phoenix going with Jy threw a monkey wrench in her plan, but she still decided to proceed anyway. Creeping her way towards the back of the house, she made sure not to make a sound. The last thing she needed was for someone to see her and call the police.

Dousing the perimeter of Phoenix's house with the paint thinner and lighter fluid, she stepped back. She put fire to her Black & Mild cigar and tossed the match to the side of the house. For a minute, she just stood there and watched the flames erupt. Then she took off running like a bolt of lightning towards her car. Jail was not a place she wanted to be, so she had to be extremely careful.

Hennessy sat back in her car as Phoenix's home lit up the sky. An evil chuckle escaped her lips, because she could imagine Phoenix's face once she saw her house in ashes. Hennessy grabbed her burner phone and placed a call to the fire department. Her plan didn't go the way she wanted it to, but she felt that what she had done was much better. Sirens were heard in the distance as Hennessy started her engine and took off down the street.

She laughed hysterically at the thought of Jy cutting up at the hospital, looking for his bald head ass mama. She couldn't stand that old bitch either, because she was partially the reason Jy had broken up with her. Belinda felt that Hennessy wasn't good enough for her son and she made sure that it was known every time Jy brought her around. Hennessy felt a sense of relief knowing that she had done what she had come to do.

Chapter Twelve

Jy rushed to park his car and jumped out of it. He ran inside of the ER in panic mode with Phoenix hot on his heels. He didn't know the severity of his mother's issues for her being brought to the hospital. He was in a frantic and panicked state as he approached the desk for information.

"MA'AM, I NEED TO KNOW WHAT ROOM BELINDA BENTON IS IN!" he said in an agitated voice as he banged on the front desk. The hood rat sat in the seat, patting her stiff weave and smacking on a piece of pink bubblegum. Jy became disgusted once she opened her mouth, exposing her rusted gold tooth. He stood back as she typed in the information, then focused her attention back to him. Brushing her tongue across her chapped lips, she smiled.

"We have no Belinda Benton here sir," she said, adding confusion to Jy's already hyped up frame of mind.

"The fuck you mean you don't have a Belinda Benton here? ONE OF THESE HOES UP IN HERE JUST FUCKING CALLED MY FUCKIN' PHONE AND SAID MY MOM WAS BROUGHT IN!" he barked. Phoenix grabbed his arm and started rubbing her hand up and down to try and calm him down. Patients in the waiting area were now focusing on the scene before them.

"I'm sorry, sir. I don't know who called you. I checked the system and we have no one here by that name."

"YOU BETTER CHECK THAT SHIT AGAIN!" he spat in a furious tone. He refused to believe that someone would play such a cruel joke on him. The girl behind the desk searched the system once again, before letting Jy down once more.

"I'm sorry, sir. I still don't see anyone by the name of Belinda Benton in our system," she said.

"FUCK!" he snapped as his fist connected with the wall. Jy stormed out of the hospital, headed back to his car and slid in.

Phoenix said nothing as her hands rubbed up and down Jy's back. She hated seeing him in such a bad mood, but the mere thought of saying anything wasn't happening. Resting her head against the leather headrest, Phoenix closed her eyes while thinking of who could have played such a mean joke on her man. They were quiet the entire ride back to her house.

"What the fuck?" Jy questioned out loud, causing Phoenix to open her eyes. She hadn't realized that she had drifted off to sleep, but jumped up when she heard Jy's tone.

The sky was lit up due to the red and blue lights that adorned Phoenix's street. All of her neighbors were outside pointing and making small talk and she wondered what had happened. The street was blocked off and Phoenix was too exhausted to sit and wait for them to clear the street, so she got out. Jy shut down his engine and joined her as they walked hand in hand towards her home. Her neighbor, Ms. Dallas, pointed and whispered while staring at her with a sympathetic look that she kindly ignored. As Phoenix and Jy grew closer to her home, an eerie feeling engulfed her.

Phoenix took off running with Jy behind her. Seeing the firefighters spraying down her home caused her knees to buckle underneath her as she fell to the ground. Tears started pouring from her eyes as Jy held her close and rocked her back and forth. She allowed him to hold her for the next ten minutes. She finally pulled herself together and rose to her feet, making her way towards the scene.

"Ma'am, you can't go over there," an officer said. Phoenix stopped and turned towards him. She wiped her face before speaking.

"THAT WAS MY HOUSE! THAT'S MY FUCKIN' HOUSE! I NEED TO KNOW WHAT THE FUCK HAPPENED TO MY DAMN HOUSE!" She spat as her eyes remained on her once beautiful home going up in flames. She couldn't stop the tears at seeing everything she had worked so hard for in a blazing inferno right before her eyes.

"One sec ma'am, my apologies for the loss of your home and personal things. Give me one second and I will have someone come and explain everything to you."

"Explain what? LOOK AT MY HOUSE! THERE'S NOTHING TO EXPLAIN!" she cried.

Jy's arm rested around Phoenix's neck as they waited for answers from the fire chief.

"How did this happen? How did this happen, Jy?" she questioned over and over, burying her face into Jy's chest. He hated that he had no answers for her, but he was thankful that she had gone with him to the hospital. He wouldn't have been able to take it had something happened to her.

"Hello ma'am, Officer Mike says you are the owner of this home," one of the firemen said as he approached them.

"Yes, can you please tell me what happened to my house?" Phoenix tried her hardest to detain her attitude, but it was getting harder each second that passed. She couldn't believe her beautiful home was engulfed in flames. How could that have happened?

"Unfortunately ma'am, from the looks of things, this wasn't an accident."

"WHAT?!" Phoenix shrieked.

"From our initial investigation, it looks like arson. It seems as though someone intentionally set fire to your home. Do you have any idea who would want to cause harm to you?" he asked.

Phoenix and Jy looked at one another with disapproving eyes. On one hand, they felt that Fredrick was responsible. But, on the other, the situation had Hennessy's name written all over it. They both looked back towards the officer and fireman before answering.

"NO!" they both said in unison.

****

Brazailia yelped as a sharp pain shot down her back. Panic and fear set in because she was all alone and had no one to call. Little Fredrick was with his father and she knew that Fredrick would make that the reason he couldn't come. She stood from her bed with an urge to pee. As she took her first step, her water broke and she immediately started feeling contractions.

"AGGGHHH!" she winced, falling back onto the bed. She started practicing the breathing techniques she had learned when she was pregnant with her son, but they weren't working. Brazailia looked over her head for her phone to no avail. Feeling around in the bed, she happened upon it and grabbed her phone to call for an ambulance.

"911, what is your emergency?"

"I... need... help," she said as she breathed the way she was taught during Lamaze classes. "I'm in labor," she said, just above a whisper. The pain she was experiencing was nothing short of excruciating.

"Hold tight ma'am. I'm going to get someone right over," the dispatcher informed her.

Brazailia threw her head back as another contraction hit her with full force. She couldn't understand why her baby girl was trying to come now when she still had eight weeks left. Struggling to get up, Brazailia slowly stood from the bed and took baby steps towards the door. Taking one step at a time, she continued down the hall until she reached the front door. Cracking the front door open, she stood against the wall. She felt at ease hearing the sirens from the ambulance growing closer. As bad as she hated it, she knew her baby girl was coming and it hurt her to the core that she would have to go through labor alone.

Once the ambulance pulled into the apartment parking lot, she grabbed her purse. She hadn't even packed an overnight bag yet, because she wasn't expecting to go in to labor two months early. She was worried that her baby wouldn't survive being born so premature. She was placed on the stretcher and into the back of the ambulance.

Once she was loaded in the ambulance, the paramedic placed the blood pressure cup on her arm. Once he did that, he checked her temperature and began taking her information. He made the call to the hospital to let them know that they were coming in with a woman in labor.

"I'm not supposed to be due yet," Brazailia cried.

"What was that?" the paramedic asked.

She removed the oxygen mask from her face and repeated, "I'm not supposed to be due yet."

"When is your due date?" he asked.

"Two months from now," she cried.

"How many weeks are you?"

"Thirty one and a half."

"Put the oxygen back on your face. Your blood pressure is through the roof," he said as he spoke into the radio. "She's only thirty one and a half weeks and her BP is extremely high!"

"We're almost there!" the other paramedic said.

"Is there anyone you want us to call?"

Brazailia didn't know who to call at that point. Because Frederick had their son, she knew he wouldn't come. Her family was in Atlanta, so she didn't have anyone else out here to call. She wanted to call Frederick, but she knew he didn't care too much about her. He had been pining for his ex-wife ever since she signed the divorce papers. He was really going crazy since he found out about her new man.

He didn't think that she would find someone that soon and he kept saying the same thing to Brazailia. She didn't want to hear about his feelings for his ex, so she decided to get her own place. She was tired watching a grown man, who she loved, whine about his ex-wife. She deserved better and she knew it. She wasn't an ugly chick, albeit a little too hood for some men. But, she was sure that she could find someone who would dig the hood in her and give her a shot.

"No, there's no one."

A few minutes later, the ambulance pulled up to the emergency room entrance. The double doors opened and a couple members of the staff came rushing out. They were worried about a pregnant woman going into labor eight weeks early. They wheeled her upstairs to the maternity and delivery floor and straight to the room. As they slid her over to the bed, the EMT's handed the paperwork to the attending staff and rushed back out.

They wrapped the baby monitor around her protruding belly and turned on the machine. They located the baby's heartbeat and then Brazailia screamed as another contraction hit her. The doctor came in and asked, "How are you feeling?"

"I'm in pain, how do you think I'm feeling?"

"Well, we called your OB and she's on her way. We're going to check to see how far along you're dilated. Did you want an epidural?" the emergency obstetrician asked.

"Yes!" she said through clenched teeth.

"Well, let's check your cervix and then we'll get an anesthesiologist in here," the doctor stated as he put a pair of gloves on. The nurse stood by and watched as he examined her vagina. She felt some kind of way about having a male doctor examine her cookies, but what could she do about it. "I'm afraid there isn't time for an epidural."

"WHAT?!" Brazailia practically screamed.

"You're already at nine centimeters, so we have to get you ready to push this baby out," the doctor said. The nurse hurried out and came back with a team of nurses. The doctor removed the bottom of the bed that Brazailia was lying in and got back between her legs. A nurse held her hand as she was instructed to push and bear down.

Brazailia pushed for the next fifteen minutes and then the doctor told her to relax. She watched as the nurse rushed over to the incubator with her tiny newborn and began doing CPR on the little one. It was hard for Brazailia to maintain her composure as she watched the nurses try to get her baby to breathe. She longed to hear her little cry, but after about ten minutes, the nurses gave up and quit doing CPR.

"WHAT ARE YOU DOING?! WHY ARE YOU STOPPING?!" Brazailia screamed.

"I'm so sorry."

"No, you can't stop! DON'T STOP!" Brazailia cried.

"I'm sorry, but there's nothing else that we can do for your baby," the nurse said with tears in her eyes.

"NOOOOOOOOO!! KEEP TRYING... SHE'LL BREATHE! I KNOW SHE WILL!" she cried. "NINA PLEASE, BREATHE FOR MOMMY, BABY! NINA PLEASE!"

The nurses looked at her with sorrow written all over their faces. "I want my baby!" she cried softly. "Please... please try again," she begged.

The nurses didn't know what to do. They had done everything they were trained to do in situations like this and couldn't get the baby to breathe. They couldn't keep doing CPR because she was too fragile. They didn't want to risk breaking a little bone on the baby, especially since she only weighed one pound.

Brazailia finally accepted that her baby girl was gone. She looked at the doctor and asked, "Was my blood pressure the reason I went into premature labor?"

"Yes, your blood pressure was way too high, especially for someone in your condition," the doctor answered as he stood up from the seat. "I'm going to prescribe you something for pain and you can go home in a couple of hours."

Brazailia felt as if her whole world had just crumbled and she knew exactly who was to blame for it...

Chapter Thirteen

"I need you to drive me to that bitch's house!" Phoenix said to Jy as they got back in his car.

"You know if you go over there, things are not gonna go well," he said.

"I don't give a fuck at this point. That bitch trashed my fuckin' car and now, she burned my house down! Am I supposed to just let her keep getting away with shit?"

"I'm not saying that, babe but…"

"BUT WHAT, JY?!"

"It's just that you don't have any proof that she was the one who did those things," he tried to reason.

"Oh, she did it alright! Who else would have done such a thing?" Phoenix asked.

"Why don't you just let the police and fire captain do their jobs?"

"I'm not waiting for her to pull another stunt! Now, you can either drive me to her house or I can call an Uber driver. Either way, I'm getting there," she said angrily.

Jy shrugged his shoulders and started the car. The last thing he wanted was for his woman and his ex to get into a fight. But, if Hennessy had something to do with Phoenix's car getting trashed and her house getting burned to the ground, it had to be settled. Against his better judgment, he drove in the direction of Hennessy's house.

When they drove up, Hennessy had just sat down to watch the news. She was anxious to see Phoenix's house up in flames or burnt to ashes. She needed to see that bitch suffer. She saw headlights pull into her driveway and peeked through the blinds. She smiled happily when she saw Jy's car in her driveway. She rushed to the bathroom to make sure she looked presentable. She applied some MAC cherry blossom glossy lipstick, took her hair out of the ponytail and sprayed some *Chanel Coco Mademoiselle*.

She was satisfied with her boy shorts and tank top as she rushed to open the door. When she did open the door to receive Jy, what she got was Phoenix grabbing her by her hair and pulling her outside. "Bitch... you... fucked... up... my... house!" For every word she spoke, she punched Hennessy in her face.

The two women rolled around on the ground, fighting like two cats. Hennessy couldn't believe that Phoenix was beating her down like that once again. She tried to get her bearings to kick her ass, but Phoenix was powered by rage and she was not stopping until she had beat Hennessy into the ground. Jy stood to the side and watched the women duke it out. He wanted to stop Phoenix, but he couldn't. He knew that Hennessy deserved everything she was getting.

Hennessy couldn't believe that Jy was just standing there watching Phoenix beat her ass. She finally managed to get the upper hand and finally got to hit Phoenix with a few hits, before Phoenix hit her with two punches, sending her flying backwards. Phoenix jumped up and ran after her. Hennessy got inside her house and slammed her door shut, clicking the lock in place.

"I'LL GET YOU FOR THAT SHIT BITCH! THIS SHIT AIN'T OVER!" Phoenix yelled.

She and Jy made their way back to his car as Hennessy fought to catch her breath. Once they had left her driveway, she slowly made her way to the bathroom. Her head was aching and so was her face. She just knew she was going to have a black eye and a stiff body in the morning. She thought about calling the police and pressing charges against Phoenix, but she didn't want to alert them to her illegal activities.

She was scared to death that the authorities would find out that she was the one responsible for Hennessy's car and house issues. There was no way she was going to spend another day in jail. And Phoenix was right, the shit was far from over.

****

"Let's see what we have cooking in there," Doctor Lewis said as she squirted ultrasound gel on Camryn's stomach. Syd stood beside her, holding her hand, ecstatic while waiting for the sex of his unborn child to be revealed. He so desperately wanted a girl, while Camryn was dead set on having a little boy.

"Come on doc, go ahead and tell her that it's a girl," Syd chuckled. Camryn rolled her eyes and said a quick prayer for a baby boy.

A brief silence lingered throughout the room as Doctor Lewis continued to rotate the wand around Camryn's stomach. Camryn and Syd stared at the doctor as they tried to read her facial expressions, but she held a blank one. She tried to find the baby's heartbeat and got the surprise of her life. Undoubtedly, it would also be the surprise of her patient's life as well. Taking a step back, she tilted her head and produced a faint smile on her face.

"Is everything aight?" Syd questioned, becoming uncomfortable with the way the doctor was stalling. The last thing he needed was for something to be wrong with his seed, especially after everything he and Camryn had been through.

"Yes, everything is perfect!" she responded happily.

"Well, what the fuck? Are we having a boy or a girl? Spit it out, doc! You got a nigga nervous as fuck over here!" he spat, tired of the games Doctor Lewis was playing.

"SYDNEY!" Camryn yelled, smacking his hand. She was shocked at the way he was acting, more so embarrassed.

"It looks to me that you have the best of both worlds growing inside of you," Doctor Lewis announced. Camryn and Syd looked at one another, confused as hell. They were trying to figure out what Doctor Lewis was saying to them.

"Can you elaborate please?" Camryn asked with her arms crossed over her chest.

"Well, it looks like you are having twins, baby A is a girl and baby B is a boy. See," she said as she pointed to the babies and took pictures of their private parts for the couple. "Congratulations!" Doctor Lewis beamed as she grabbed a napkin and proceeded to wipe the gel off of Camryn's stomach. Syd started breathing heavy as he clenched his chest. He was baffled at the fact that he had become a father of three so quickly.

"Alright Miss Peters, stop out front and schedule your next appointment. Everything looks good and congrats again. Oh, and here are your sonogram pictures," she rattled as she handed them the slew of pictures she had printed for them. She grabbed her clipboard and made her way out the door. Syd and Camryn sat quietly, still in shock at the latest news. She was happy that she had kept her babies, but fear engulfed her as she realized that she would soon be the mother of two.

"How you feel?" Syd questioned, taking a seat. He nervously wiped his sweaty palms on the legs of his Balmain jeans.

"I'm speechless! How the hell did we end up with two damn babies, Syd? Ain't that much fucking in the world! I can't believe this shit," she hissed, resting her palm against her forehead. She became jittery as butterflies started floating around in her stomach. Syd grabbed her hand to help her off of the table. They walked out of the exam room, hand in hand, saying nothing to one another. Camryn wouldn't admit it to Syd, but she was afraid. Afraid that she would fail her kids, because she didn't have the slightest clue on how to take care of one, let alone two.

Once Camryn's next appointment was made, they made their way to Syd's car.

"I see somebody finally got their happily ever after. Your sorry ass hasn't been over to see Junior in damn near two weeks. Don't tell me that he's become non-existent to you because this bitch is pregnant. I'm happy to finally see the bitch that mistreated my kid though," Ursula said. She was the last person that Syd and Camryn expected to see when they walked out of the doctor's office. How the hell did she even know they were there?

Ursula turned her attention to Camryn and began to address her, "Now, I could care less about Syd being with you. Shit, have at it! But, what you won't do is fuck up his relationship with his kid!" Ursula spat as she watched Syd interact with Camryn. She had finally shaken the love bug inside of her, but she would be damned if she allowed Syd to neglect their son for some bougie ass bitch.

"Hold up, first off..." Syd cut Camryn off.

"Urs, don't start no dumb shit! I would never neglect my son and you know that shit! I just saw my lil nigga two days ago, so what the fuck yo ass been smokin'?" Syd looked at Camryn and saw the angry expression she held on her beautiful face. They had just gotten back together and baby mama drama was the last thing he needed.

"Whatever! I need you to get him this weekend, because I have shit to do!" she snapped as she walked off. Truth be told, she was tired of Junior's lil ass and she desperately needed another break. Syd had asked her to keep him for a couple of days, not a couple of weeks. Junior was a thorn in her side that she desperately needed to get out.

Syd shook his head in disgust as he opened the door for Camryn to slide in. Making his way to the driver's side, he hopped in and started the engine. Camryn had yet to say anything and that alone made him nervous.

"You can bring your son to my house if you want. I won't sit here and act as if I'm not pissed off about that bitch just popping up out of nowhere, because I am. But this wasn't your fault. You can grab your shit from her spot while you're at it; there's no reason it should still be there.

Ursula was right and I am grown enough to admit it. I should have never treated Junior the way that I did, because he is innocent in all of this. As an educator who spends eight hours a day with kids who aren't mine I actually feel ashamed of my behavior and I'm sorry."

Syd was shocked, yet turned on by Camryn's words. He sat back in his seat and admired the way her arms were folded at the top of her stomach. Her bottom lip poked out while she breathed heavily.

"My shit ain't at her spot. I haven't stayed with Ursula in months, ma. I have my own spot," he confessed. Camryn swallowed the lump in her throat, feeling like a fool. Her heart smiled knowing that Syd hadn't been staying with his baby mama the whole time they had been apart. She was almost certain that he had gone back to Ursula when they split, so to know that he hadn't was a major relief.

"Hmm, that's good to hear. Can we go though, I'm hungry as hell," she said, pulling the seat belt around her and snapping it in place.

"What you and those greedy ass babies wanna eat now? Your ass just ate before we got here," he chuckled. He couldn't wait for his kids to be born so that his family would be complete. His heart yearned for Camryn to bear his kids and share his last name. When they split, he worried that it would never happen. Another woman would have never sufficed if he couldn't have Camryn. For four months, he had been celibate because deep down, he knew that Camryn would come back. He would never betray her the way he had years ago. She meant just that much to him.

"I'm not bringing Junior over if you're going to mistreat him, ma. I love you, Cam; God knows I do. But, you have to accept my son as you accept me. Ain't no way around that shit," he hissed.

"Understood," she simply said as he pulled into traffic.

Chapter Fourteen

Brazailia sat in the hospital bed in a traumatic state following the death of her baby. She found it extremely hard to accept that her baby girl was really gone. She had been in the hospital for the past three days and Frederick hadn't called or anything. It was odd that he had their son, but never tried to check up on her when he knew she was pregnant with their daughter. Today was the day she would be going home, but she didn't want to. Going home without Nina was something she dreaded. Seeing the Minnie Mouse nursery that she had decorated for her baby girl was going to be unbearable.

"Okay Miss Floyd, here are your discharge papers and instructions on caring for your stitches. Once again, I am sorry for your loss," the nurse said as she handed Brazailia her paperwork. Brazailia grabbed her papers and slowly stood from the bed. Her heart ached looking down at her once pregnant belly and she sobbed lightly.

"Lord, why am I suffering like this?" she asked no one in particular as she searched for answers. She knew not to question God, but she wanted to know why her baby couldn't be with her. She had finally come to terms with becoming a mother again, so she didn't understand why her baby girl had to be taken away.

Brazailia slowly sat in the wheelchair and the nurse pushed her towards the elevator. She could tell the young woman was struggling with losing her baby, which was why the doctors kept her admitted for three days. They wanted to monitor her and make sure she was well enough to go home alone. Brazailia sat in the wheelchair with tear filled eyes and a heavy heart. Her knees felt weak, so she was glad that she was being wheeled around.

The pain of losing a child was something she wouldn't wish on anyone and the fact that she had to do it all alone, stabbed at her soul. Frederick didn't have the slightest clue as to what had been going on with Brazailia. She had called him numerous times to tell him that she had lost the baby, but he hadn't answered. He hated her just that much.

The pain that she was feeling, she wanted Frederick to feel three times worse. She was tired of being second best when it came to him stressing over Phoenix. She felt that she had done her part and done it well, but it still wasn't enough.

"Is someone coming to get you?" the nurse asked.

"No, it's okay. I'll take the bus," Brazailia said.

"Are you sure there isn't anyone that you can call?"

"I said I'll be fine," Brazailia responded, this time with a little more attitude.

"Okay…" the nurse said as she raised her hands in surrender.

Once they got to the first floor, Brazailia stepped out of the wheelchair and proceeded to walk out the door. Her body ached for the loss of her daughter and her legs quaked with each step she took. Stepping onto the concrete outside the hospital, the heat immediately hit her. She checked her bag for some change and headed towards the bus stop. Her walk showed just how much pain she was in. As Brazailia approached the bus stop, an orange

Lamborghini approached her. As the windows rolled down, she rolled her eyes once she saw Phoenix's face. Her body held no energy to argue with the woman she was competing with.

Phoenix's eyes became glossy as she looked at Brazailia. She couldn't stand Brazailia, but seeing her looking so frail and meek, kinda tugged at her heartstrings. She could tell that something was wrong and noticed that Brazailia was crying, even though she tried to wipe those tears away when she saw Phoenix.

"Is everything okay? Do you need a ride?" Phoenix asked. A quick store run had quickly turned into a 'Captain Save a Ho' mission.

"Umm, yeah," Brazailia hesitantly responded. She hated that she needed Phoenix at the moment, but her options were slim. She definitely didn't belong on a bus in her current state. Sitting among those people on those nasty seats that never got cleaned was not what she needed at the moment. She walked over to the passenger's side and heard Phoenix unlock the door.

Brazailia slid in the smooth, buttery seat of the expensive car and buckled her seat belt.

"Thank you!" she said before the tears started rolling. Phoenix pulled over into the Super Walmart parking lot and turned to look at Brazailia. As much as she didn't like the girl, she did have compassion for her.

"Please don't tell me that nigga left you out here with two kids to fend for by yourself." Phoenix was livid, thinking the worst of her ex-husband. Brazailia bawled her eyes out in front of Phoenix and she hated that she was so vulnerable. She didn't want to look like a weak bitch in front of the woman Fred continued to pine over.

"I would rather him had done that instead of what he actually did do."

"Oh my! What did he do?" Phoenix asked.

"I went into premature labor a few nights ago," Brazailia admitted as tears continued to fall.

"Oh my God! Is your baby okay?"

"Noooo!" Brazailia said as her voice quivered. "She was too small and underdeveloped, so she… she… she didn't make it!" She burst into tears and Phoenix didn't know what else to do but try to comfort the girl. Phoenix rubbed her back as she cried.

"I'm so sorry that happened to you. Has Frederick been to see you? I mean, why didn't he pick you up to take you home? You shouldn't be riding the bus in your condition, because you run the risk of getting an infection."

"I called him several times, too many to count. He actually has our son, but he won't answer any of my calls. He doesn't even know that I lost the baby. I hate him! I hate him so much Phoenix," she continued to cry, which angered Phoenix.

How could a man she once loved so much be so insensitive? Sure, Brazailia was a little rough around the edges. Hell, up until now, Phoenix didn't even like her ass. But, no woman deserved to be treated the way she had been by any man. Phoenix reached in her handbag and grabbed her phone. She quickly dialed Frederick's number. She was so upset that her hands were shaking as she waited for her ex-husband to answer her call.

"Hey baby…" he answered in excitement.

"Nah motherfucker, don't baby me…" she said angrily.

"What are you talking about? Why are you so angry?"

"Why haven't you answered Brazailia's calls?" she asked.

"What?!" Frederick couldn't believe his ex-wife was asking him questions about his baby mama. What the hell did Phoenix care about Brazailia? The two of them didn't even like each other so why was she worried about his baby mama?

"You heard me, nigga! That girl called you a buncha times… why didn't you answer?"

"Why you asking me about my baby mama? That don't concern you. Let's talk about us and getting back…"

Phoenix already knew where he was going with this conversation, so she cut him off. "WHAT DON'T YOU UNDERSTAND?! THERE IS NO US! THERE WILL NEVER BE AN US EVER AGAIN IN THIS LIFETIME OR THE NEXT!" Phoenix was so frustrated with Frederick at that point.

"Then why don't you tell me what you want because I got shit to do," he said with an instant attitude.

"I got shit to do too, motherfucker! Lemme ask you something… did you even know that Brazailia went into premature labor a few days ago? Huh? Huh nigga? Did you know?"

"What are you talking about? She ain't due for another two months," he said.

"That's why I asked if you knew she went into premature labor, DUMMY!"

"So, she had the baby. What hospital she in?" he asked, sounding uninterested.

"She's not in the hospital anymore, ASS! She was discharged today! YOU SHOULD HAVE BEEN THERE FOR HER! YOU SHOULD HAVE BEEN THERE TO DRIVE HER HOME INSTEAD OF HER WAITING AT A FUCKIN' BUS STOP! HOW COULD YOU BE SO FUCKIN' INSENSITIVE?!" Phoenix yelled. She couldn't believe this man that she used to love so much was treating that girl the way that he was.

"They let the baby go home already?" he asked.

"Oh, now you're concerned. She lost the baby, idiot!!"

Frederick didn't know that. He didn't know that was the reason for Brazailia's constant and incessant calls. He was so aggravated with her. That was why he didn't want to speak with her. He got tired of her whining and bitching. But, had he known that she had lost the baby, he would have answered.

"Where is she?"

"Why the fuck you asking me? You are such an ass. I don't know what we ever saw in you!" Phoenix said as she ended the call.

Brazailia couldn't believe the woman she once couldn't stand was sticking up for her. She couldn't believe that she was actually showing her compassion and support. "What's your address?" Phoenix asked.

"Thank you," Brazailia said with tears in her eyes.

"For what?"

"For making that call."

"Girl bye… it felt good to go off on his ass! I'd do it again if I needed to. Just know that you can do better. Just because you have a child with Frederick, doesn't mean you have to put up with his bullshit! You deserve someone who treats you with love and respect and he ain't that nigga, ya heard me?" Phoenix said as Brazailia cracked a smile.

"You're right. I do deserve better. I'm gonna start looking out for me and mine and that's it."

"Good for you," Phoenix said as she started the car and they headed to Brazailia's apartment.

Once they arrived, Brazailia thanked Phoenix again before getting out of the car. Phoenix smiled to herself at having helped Brazailia. After everything she had been through over the past few days, she realized that it hadn't been that bad compared to what Brazailia had been going through. That old saying that her grandmother used to say rang true. Her grandmother used to say, "Baby, no matter how bad you think you have it, there's always somebody that has it worse than you."

That was so true. She had lost her house and her Jeep had been trashed, but those were material things that could be replaced. Brazailia lost a child and no matter what she did, she could never get her baby back.

****

Frederick had been trying to reach Brazailia ever since Phoenix had gone off on him. She was supposed to get their son back three days ago, but she hadn't been picking up her phone. Frederick enjoyed spending time with his son, but he had to work. He didn't have any family out here so he didn't know who he could leave his son with if he couldn't find Brazailia. He decided to go to her apartment and just knock on her door. He had to go to work so she needed to stop whatever she was doing and take their son. He knew that she was going through something following the miscarriage, but damn. He had shit to do!

Why the hell did I ever get involved with her project ass anyway, he wondered. He pulled into her complex parking lot and saw her lil car parked near her apartment. He got out of the car and took his son out of the car seat. He carried his son in his arms as he approached the door. He knocked on it and waited for her to answer. He knocked again… and again… and again, but she never responded.

"Where the hell is your stupid ass mama?" he muttered to his young son.

He peeked through the windows and saw Brazailia lying on the sofa, staring at the television. He knocked on the window.

TAP! TAP! TAP!

"BRAZAILIA! BRAZAILIA! I KNOW YOU FUCKIN' HEAR ME, GIRL! OPEN THIS DAMN DOOR!" Frederick yelled from outside the front door.

Brazailia heard Frederick knocking outside her apartment and couldn't believe he had the nerve to show up at her place. What the fuck was he doing here?

Strutting towards her front door, Brazailia swung her door open and stared intensely at Frederick. She tried to smile at their baby boy, because she was happy to see him. Regardless of how she felt about his daddy, that had nothing to do with their son.

"WHY THE HELL ARE YOU BEATING ON MY GOTDAMN DOOR LIKE THAT AND WHAT DO YOU WANT?!" she spat angrily. It was Frederick's intention to come and apologize for the way he had treated her, but she was pushing it.

"You never came to pick up Fabian and you knew I had shit to do. See… that's that bullshit I be talking about!" he spat further, fueling the already blazing fire that she held inside. Brazailia snatched their son inside and ordered him to go to his room while she talked with his father. She watched as Fabian ascended the stairs before turning her focus back to the task at hand.

"You have some nerve bringing your ain't shit ass over here, talking shit when I couldn't even get you to bring your ass to the hospital. I'm so over you and your desperate pleas for attention. Phoenix don't even want your ass nigga, so get over it!" she hissed with her hand resting on her hip. Her blood boiled hotter each second that Frederick stood in her presence. Rage emanated through her pores while he held a smile, further raising the bar of her anger.

"What happened to Nina?" he asked, trying to throw her off from the matter at hand.

Brazailia chuckled before sizing him up and down.

"Don't ask me shit about MY daughter. You didn't give a damn about her anyways." Brazailia walked away from the door with Frederick following her every move. He wasn't done talking, nor did he plan on allowing her to speak the last word. He knew he was wrong for not being there, but at the same time, his pride wouldn't allow him to bow down when she no longer meant anything to him. If he was honest with himself, he would have to admit that Brazailia never meant anything to him. She was just a distraction while he tried to get the problems with his wife off his mind.

"I'm sorry for letting you go through that alone, but maybe it was for the best. We both knew that having another baby wasn't the best idea for neither of us." Brazailia looked at Frederick as if he had two heads. Her eyes turned black while her right eye twitched. How dare Frederick speak such ill words about her deceased child! The pain she felt shooting through her body only made matters worse as she slowly opened the kitchen drawer. Frederick continued to rant about how Nina would only confuse the public on the status of their relationship. It was bad enough he had to deal with Brazailia when it came to Fabian and having another baby would have only added insult to injury.

"You know what pisses me off when it comes to you Frederick?" she asked with her back facing him. "No matter how much I did for you, no matter what I took from you, you still felt the need to give me your ass to kiss. I loved you... even though loving you did nothing but kill me. I took shit from you that wasn't normal on any level. I was your side bitch when you didn't deserve it. Now, you bring your stupid ass in my house and tell me that my daughter was a mistake. YOU BASTARD! I HATE YOUR ENTIRE EXISTENCE!"

Brazailia blanked out and turned around swiftly, plunging the knife into Frederick's chest. He winced in pain as she extracted the knife and inserted it repeatedly. Frederick's legs became weak as he slowly fell to the floor. Trepidation engulfed her as soon as she snapped back to reality. Her heart rate skyrocketed as she watched Frederick's chest struggle to rise and fall.

"OH GOD! OH MY GOD! WHAT DID I DO?!" she questioned as she frantically jumped over Frederick's body. He took his last breath as his head fell to the side with his eyes wide open.

Chapter Fifteen

Drew packed the last of his things as he scanned his office. He couldn't believe his life had come to this, but he knew that he couldn't blame anyone but himself. Once Camryn exposed his sex life to his wife, Jessica made it her business to go to the board and rat him out. She disclosed information to the board of education that also landed Tucker in the unemployment office. Not because they were gay, but because they were fraternizing in the work place, as well as committing adultery, which the board frowned upon. There was a morals clause in their contracts that they clearly violated with their extracurricular activities.

As if that wasn't enough to ruin his life, she filed for a divorce and hired the best divorce lawyer in Baton Rouge. She was fighting for everything he had. Drew felt that he had failed not only his marriage, but he felt like shit for breaking his vows to God. The worse thing about this entire situation was that he had let his kids down. They were the most innocent ones and he had failed them when he broke his marriage vows. It hurt him to know that people were talking about him and his family behind their backs and snickering to their faces.

Grabbing the large cardboard box from his desk, Drew walked out of his office with his head down, filled with embarrassment. He caught a glimpse of Mrs. Richardson snickering as he walked by her office. His feelings were a little hurt by her actions. He always thought that the two of them worked well together. He couldn't believe she was behaving that way.

"Keep it on the down low… nobody has to know!" She sang out loud as she snapped her fingers on one hand while waving the LGBT flag in the air with the other. "Hey Drew, why don't you hit the booty-doo for us. Shake ya ass, watch ya self, shake ya ass, show us whatcha working with!" Mrs. Richardson was laughing so hard, she had to catch her chest to catch her breath. Drew wouldn't dare let Mrs. Richardson get under his skin before, but now that he had been terminated, he felt that he would give her a piece of his mind.

"You have so much to say about my sexuality, you old battle axe bitch! But, what you need to do is reevaluate your own marriage. That husband you so dearly cherish has just as much of a unicorn booty as the next." Frederick laughed hysterically while whistling as Mrs. Richardson's mouth hung wide open.

She tried not to let what Drew had said bother her, but it was all she was able to think about for the rest of the day. She couldn't wait to get home to snoop around and find out if what Drew had insinuated about her beloved husband was true. Nine out of ten, she knew she didn't have anything to worry about. She knew that Drew was just trying to get under her skin, but she wasn't about to let him.

She had been married to her husband for over thirty years. She knew him like she knew the back of her hand. She decided that Drew was just being petty and didn't give it another thought. When Camryn walked in the office to check her mailbox, Mrs. Richardson couldn't wait to tell her the news.

"My, my... aren't you getting big!" she remarked.

Camryn just rolled her eyes at Mrs. Richardson, because she was not in the mood for any kind of bullshit from the old lady. "What can I do for you, Mrs. Richardson?" she asked.

"I just wanted to know if you had seen the drama with Principal Drew this morning," Mrs. Richardson said.

"No… whatever Drew has going on in his life has nothing to me. As you can see," Camryn said as she rubbed her seven month pregnant belly. "I have enough going on in my own life."

"I understand that. How much longer do you have left before you drop? You are huge!"

"Well, that's what normally happens when women are expecting twins," Camryn responded sarcastically. "I have eleven weeks left, but this week is my last week. The doctor wants me on bed rest for the rest of my pregnancy."

"Wow! So, are you and the baby's daddy gonna tie the knot? I mean, I don't see any ring on that pretty little finger of yours," Mrs. Richardson commented.

Camryn stopped going through her mail and looked at the old meddling woman up and down before responding. "Mrs. Richardson, I've tried my best to be as respectful as I can to your old ass, but you make shit impossible. Instead of worrying about my business, why not worry about your own? Did you know that your husband has been creeping around with Lucy Perez?"

Camryn hated to be the bearer of bad news, but she was tired of Mrs. Richardson and her nosy ass. What business was it of hers if she and her baby's daddy got married or not? None of that had anything to do with her. She had the information concerning Mr. Richardson a long time ago, but kept it to herself because it wasn't her business or her place. But, Mrs. Richardson had been pushing her luck for the longest time and she had enough.

"What are you talking about?" she asked.

"I'm talking about your husband and Lucy Perez meeting at the Motel 6 on Reiger Road. I bet if you go there now, he will be there," Camryn said.

Mrs. Richardson's face got flushed and she looked like she was ready to pass out. Camryn just walked away and headed back to her classroom. She saw Tucker heading her way with a box in his hand and just kept walking. She didn't have two words for the fruity nigga. She walked in her classroom and sat behind her desk.

Tucker walked in right behind her. "Did you hear that I got fired?" he asked.

She let out an exasperated breath and asked, "What the hell does that have to do with me?"

"I just can't believe they fired me. I lost my job, my wife, everything."

"Why are you here? What are you telling me that shit for? What you got going on in your life does not concern me at all!" Camryn said as she rubbed her belly. "Look, you need to get the hell out of my classroom before you raise my blood pressure."

"Camryn, after all we've been through, how can you just…"

"Hey babe!" Syd said as he walked in her classroom. "Man, what the fuck that nigga doing in here?"

"I'm trying to figure that out myself," she responded as she stayed in her seat.

Syd turned to face Tucker and asked, "Yo bruh, don't you have somewhere to be? I'm sure they got a booty hole somewhere looking for your attention."

Syd cracked a smile as Tucker's face reflected disgust. He hated to think that Camryn and her man had been discussing him. Hell, everybody in town was talking about him and Drew. He looked at Camryn who sat in her chair looking unbothered and said, "Sorry to have bothered you, Miss Peters."

"Aye yo," Syd called after him before he walked out. "Stay away from her."

Tucker didn't respond as he continued to walk out the building with his head down. He had never been so embarrassed in all his life. What did he have left after this?

****

Hennessy hated that her plan to take out Phoenix didn't work. Not only didn't her plan work, but it failed miserably. Phoenix was now living with Jy and that was something that she couldn't fathom. How could something she wanted have backfired so badly? She didn't understand how she was going to be able to get Jy back now. She was sure that the two of them were doing the same things that she longed to do with him again. Just the thought had her going crazy.

She never intended for the two of them to live happily ever after, but she would deal with them later. She had something else to take care of at the moment. She looked at the time on the dash and saw that it was a little after two. She knew that all the dancers were gone and the only one that was left inside Club Lush was Dollar. Besides, the only vehicle on the lot was Dollar's black on black Lincoln Navigator. She cringed when she thought about his grimy hands all over her. She hated that dude for mistreating her the way that he did.

It was time for Dollar to learn a lesson. Once again, she looked around to make sure no one was watching, before exiting her car. She popped the trunk and grabbed the can of paint thinner and lighter fluid. She made her way to the rear of the building, where she knew Dollar's office was located. She was going to make sure she did this job the right way.

She dumped the paint thinner all around the back side of the building then sprayed lighter fluid everywhere. She grabbed a match, struck it along the box, then tossed it against the spot where she had sprayed the flammable liquids. The building immediately became covered in blue flames. She rushed back over to her to her car and hopped in. She waited to see when Dollar would come rushing out of the building, fighting to breathe. She waited for five minutes, but he never came out.

She moved her car to an area she felt would be inconspicuous enough to hide her vehicle. A few minutes later, she heard sirens in the distance. She smiled at the thought of Dollar finally getting what he deserved.

Chapter Sixteen

The Next Day...

Phoenix sat on the toilet, sulking in her misery as she stared at the First Response pregnancy test she held in her hands. Her hands shook vigorously while the tears fell from her eyes non-stop. She couldn't believe she had slipped up and gotten pregnant. She couldn't blame anyone but herself, because she and Jy had been so careless. Her divorce had just been finalized and she felt like a fool for getting pregnant so soon. Even though she had no reason to believe that Jy wouldn't be there for her, a part of her still felt like a baby would burden Jy.

"BABY, I'M ABOUT TO RUN OUT RIGHT QUICK... YOU GOOD?" Jy asked from the other side of the door. Phoenix took a deep breath before opening the door, allowing him to see her face. Jy stood still for a moment as Phoenix looked into his eyes.

"What's up?" he questioned. Phoenix extended her arm, handing him the test with her head down. She silently counted for the moment he could react and tell her to get an abortion the way he had done with Hennessy.

"The fuck you all sad for and shit? This is a blessing!" he snapped excitedly. Phoenix's head snapped in shock as she stared at Jy. He pulled her towards him and hugged her tight while raining kisses all over her face. Then, Jy grabbed Phoenix's stomach while looking at her. Phoenix was everything he had ever wanted in a woman and he wouldn't have wanted any other woman to bear his first child.

"I was scared," she confessed, attempting to look down, but Jy grabbed her face.

"Scared of what, ma?"

"I thought you would tell me to get an abortion, like you did with Vanessa."

"Vanessa isn't responsible enough to have any kid of mine. I fuck with you ma, matter of fact, I love your boughetto ass. I would never ask that of you because you've shown me time and time again that you're who I want to be with." Jy grabbed both sides of Phoenix's face and kissed her succulent lips. He didn't know what it was or how it happened, but he fell deeply in love with Phoenix.

Exiting the bathroom, Jy laid Phoenix on the bed and stripped her out of her clothing. Wasting no time, he buried his face in between her legs and put his tongue to work. Phoenix's hands found their way into Jy's dreads as she started to massage his hair while he pleased her. Jy loved when she did that shit. Phoenix's hands were magical to him. His dick became fully erect in a matter of seconds.

"Oouu yeeeesssss Jy, right there! That's it, baby!" She hissed as her back arched while riding the wave of Jy's tongue. She threw her pussy back each time his tongue entered her center. Her climax was near before her phone started to ring... repeatedly. She didn't have the slightest clue as to who could be calling, but the euphoric feeling that she was enduring wouldn't allow her to even worry about it.

Jy slurped and sucked all of her juices while they saturated the sheets before standing up. He removed his pants and boxers before placing himself between her legs.

"I can't wait to get in this pregnant pussy… I heard that shit is the best," he said as he entered her slowly. Jy gasped at the feeling of Phoenix's sugar walls clamping down on his dick as he thrust in and out of her. The feeling was amazing to him, so amazing, his eyes were rolling to the back of his head.

An immaculate love session was in progress as they made love, their skin slapping against one another, making their own sweet melodies. They came in unison as Jy collapsed beside her. They were both out of breath as they laid silently, their hearts smiling profusely.

Phoenix stood from the bed as Jy's phone started blaring loudly.

"Yo!" he answered out of breath.

"Aye man, the fuck y'all doing over there?" Syd asked, but before Jy had a chance to respond, Syd continued, "Never mind, just turn on the TV." Hennessy's face was all over the news and Syd wanted them to see it firsthand.

"A fire erupted at the elusive Club Lush Gentleman's Lounge late last night. A body, which has been identified as that of the club's owner, Lionel "Dollar" Barba was recovered among the burnt rubble. The body, which had been completely incinerated, was identified by dental records. A suspect has been arrested in the case. Vanessa Scott, a dancer at the club, was arrested last night and charged with arson and first degree murder. Miss Scott was arrested after fleeing the scene of the crime. Evidence was collected on Miss Scott's person, but the investigation is still ongoing. We will keep you informed as more news on the case comes to light. This is Scott Forbes, reporting for WBRZ News," the reporter said.

Phoenix and Jy stared at one another in shock. Phoenix knew that Hennessy was responsible for what had happened to her house and car, but she could replace those things since she had insurance on both. She just never thought the woman would take it as far as she had; to start another fire and kill someone in the process.

"Y'all see that shit?!" Syd asked as he spoke into the phone.

"Yea man, that shit crazy!" Jy said.

"You telling me! That muthafucka really has some fuckin' screws loose, bro!"

"Well, lemme holla atcha later, bruh." Jy and Syd ended their call and he turned to Phoenix. "Do you think they will find out that she was the one that burned your house down?"

"I hope so, but I don't think it'll make a difference. I mean, she's going to jail for burning down Lush and killing Dollar. What more can they do to her?" Phoenix asked.

"Well, let's not worry about her anymore. I just found out I'm gonna be a daddy, so let's go out and celebrate," he suggested.

"Okay, I'd like that," she said with a huge smile as she planted a kiss on his lips.

"What do you feel like eating?"

"Anything… I just love food and I'm hungry. Thanks to you, I worked up a huge appetite," she smiled.

"Well, how about we go to the steakhouse?"

"That's fine. I could use some steak and potatoes."

"Cool, let's go take a shower and get ready," Jy said.

"You know if we get in this shower together, we may never make it there…"

He scooped her up and kissed her. "That's a chance I'm willing to take," he said. "I love you Candace."

"I love you too, baby."

Phoenix had prayed for happiness like this and now that Hennessy was out of the way, she felt that she could finally get her happily ever after. Before they made it to the bathroom, Phoenix's phone began to ring. Jy looked at her and let out an exasperated sigh.

"I could just let it ring," she said.

"Nah, it might be an emergency," he said.

He put Phoenix on her feet and she went to answer her phone. She looked at the screen and didn't recognize the number. She hesitantly swiped the phone to answer it. "Hello?"

"Candace," came a soft voice over the phone.

"Who is this?" Phoenix asked.

"It's Brazailia."

Phoenix had given Brazailia her phone number in case she needed a pep talk, but never expected her to call. "What can I do for you?" she asked. Jy looked at her and mouthed, "Who is it?"

She mouthed back, "Frederick's baby mama."

"What the fuck?" he asked.

She shrugged her shoulders and waited for Brazailia to tell her why she was calling.

"Candace, can you please come over to my place?"

"Why... what's up?"

Phoenix didn't know the girl like that. She didn't know if it was a setup or something.

"Something awful happened!"

Phoenix could hear the panic in Brazailia's voice and wondered what was going on.

"What happened? Are you okay?" she asked.

"No!" Brazailia responded as she started to cry. "Can you please come over?"

"Ohhh-kay, I'm leaving now," she said as she ended the call.

"What's going on?" Jyri asked.

"I don't know. That was Brazailia and she asked could I come over. She said that something happened, but didn't tell me what."

"Are you gonna go over there?"

"Yea, will you come with me?" Phoenix asked.

"Shit, try and stop me," he said as they began to throw on some clothes.

When they were done getting dressed, Phoenix grabbed her handbag and they headed out the door. The last thing she expected to interrupt her night with her man was a phone call from Brazailia. But the real shock came when they entered her apartment. Seeing all the blood surrounding Frederick's lifeless body on her kitchen floor took Phoenix's breath away. She passed out instantly.

****

Vicious, who was now going by her real name, Rhianna had decided she was going to move past her issues with Phoenix and Fendi. She was going to take her mom's advice and put the past behind her. She was on her laptop enrolling in school. She thought it was time to get back on track with her education, so she decided to major in accounting since she had always been good with numbers.

"Rhianna! RHIANNA!" her mom called from the living room.

She jumped up from the bed and ran out of her room. "What mom? Why are you yelling like that?"

"Look!" she said as she took the television off of pause. There was a news segment about Hennessy and how she had been arrested for arson and murder. She gasped and covered her mouth at the shock of seeing her ex-friend's mug shot on the news. She couldn't believe that Hennessy had stooped so low.

"Now do you see? Now do you see why I said to move on with your life and forget all that bullshit! You don't wanna end up like that crazy ass bitch, because she's going to spend the rest of her life in jail," her mom said.

"I definitely understand," Rhianna said. "I was just signing up for school. I'm enrolling at LSU and going to study accounting."

"Good for you! I'm proud of you, baby!"

"Thanks mom and thanks for your support," Rhianna said as she hugged her mom and went back to her room to complete her sign up.

She was glad that she had decided to get her mind right. She was actually excited about going to college. She was only 26, so she was still young enough to make a difference in her life. There was one thing she needed to do so she could free all her little demons. She grabbed her purse and keys and headed out the house. She hopped in her car and made her way to the school.

When she got there, she parked her car and headed inside.

"Hello, can I help you?" the receptionist asked.

"I'm here to see Fendi… I mean, Camryn Peters," Rhianna said.

"You're just in time. She was getting ready to leave to start her maternity leave," the woman informed her.

"Is she available?"

"I think so. Let me page her," the woman said as she stood up from her seat. Before she could page for

Camryn, she walked into the front office. Her jolly smile that she had from the surprise baby shower that she was given was quickly replaced by a frown upon seeing Vicious.

"Oh, Miss Peters, I was just about to page you for your visitor!"

"What do you want?" Camryn asked as she placed some of the gifts on the table. Syd walked in and rolled his eyes towards Rhianna.

"What the hell she doing here?" he asked.

"I'm trying to find that out," Camryn responded.

"I promise you that I didn't come to start any trouble."

"You better not, because you start anything with her, I promise you today... I'm getting in yo ass!" Syd threatened.

"Fen... Camryn, I owe you an apology. I know that the shit I've done in the past won't easily be forgotten, but I'm so sorry." She began to reach in her bag, making Camryn a little nervous. But, she pulled out an envelope and handed it to Camryn.

"What's in it... anthrax?" Camryn asked.

"I deserve that," Rhianna said with a faint smile. "But, it's the money that I owe you for damaging your car. I'm sorry I did that. I was acting childish and what I did was disrespectful to you and your property."

Camryn stared at her, unable to believe that the woman she had beef with for so long was finally behaving like a human being. Syd took the envelope from her and opened it. He handed it to Camryn and she took it and looked inside. "What made you do this?" Camryn asked.

"It's just time for me to grow up. I'm sorry and I hope you will accept my apology."

Camryn studied her for a moment before she said, "Thank you and I do."

"Thanks. Congratulations on your pregnancy! I'm gonna get out of your hair now. Thanks for hearing me out," Rhianna said as she left the front office.

Camryn looked at Syd and asked, "What just happened here?"

"Sshhiiddd, her ass probably saw the news about Hennessy's triflin' ass!" Syd responded as they laughed. The two of them carried the remainder of her gifts to the truck, she said her goodbyes, and they left.

Little did she know that Syd had an even bigger surprise for her once they got back home.

Chapter Seventeen

Camryn's eyes were covered as Syd walked around to open her car door. She was nervous, yet anxious to see what he had in store for her. Since they had been back together, life had been nothing short of amazing. Camryn was more than happy and the fact that her best friend was equally happy, made her feel that much better. She couldn't wait for them to raise their kids together.

"Can you hurry up Syd? I have to piss. Why did I have to wear this anyway?" she questioned, wiggling as she tried not to pee on herself. Her bladder was her babies' favorite place to be.

Syd opened the door and stepped in front of Camryn, holding her hand. White and red rose petals adorned the floors. *Promise* by Jagged Edge played softly while vanilla scented candles burned on the mantle. Syd hit play on the projector as pictures of him and Camryn throughout the years showed on the wall. Removing the blindfold from Camryn's eyes, Syd stood back while Camryn looked around the room in awe. She admired his gesture and couldn't stop smiling.

"Baby, you did this for me?" she asked in awe.

"Of course. You deserve this and so much more."

"It's so beautiful," she said as a lone tear slipped from her eye. Syd held her stomach as he planted a kiss upon her lips.

"I'm happy you like it, ma… only the best for you."

Camryn walked in and sat on the couch as the beautiful pictures of their lives continued to play on the projector. Syd had never gone out of his way to make her smile like this and she loved it. She held her stomach as her smile grew wider with each picture.

"Oh shit, I'm about to piss on myself!" she confessed as she struggled to get up. Syd grabbed her hand and helped her up before dropping down on one knee. Camryn's hand flew towards her mouth as Syd pulled out a red velvet box. Opening the box, Camryn gasped at the yellow princess cut diamond ring.

"Baby, I don't want to go another day being just your boyfriend. We have fought battles against the strongest demons, but we conquered that shit with our heads held high. I have never met a woman as beautiful, smart, loving, and caring as you. You put my needs before yours, even when I didn't ask you to." Camryn wiggled from side to side, trying to control her bladder but she was in a tight spot. "You took me back when I know I didn't deserve it. I could go on and on, but I just got one question… will you marry a nigga and make me the happiest man on earth?"

"Baby I-"

Camryn's words got caught in her throat when the gushy, amniotic fluid rained down her legs. Syd jumped from the floor and grabbed his stomach, feeling as if he had to throw up.

"Fuck! My water broke," Camryn said nervously.

"We have to get you to the hospital, ma," Syd seethed, starting to panic.

Grabbing her bag from by the door, Syd helped Camryn to the car. Peeling out of the driveway, Syd drove like a bat out of hell while Camryn sat in the passenger seat doing her breathing techniques.

"I know you're in pain ma, but I still want my answer," he said as he weaved through traffic.

"Ye... yes baby... I will marry... ahhhh... you!" Camryn had made his day more than she knew. She was now his fiancée and she was giving birth to his seeds. Life couldn't have gotten any better than at that moment.

Epilogue...

Nine Months Later...

Camryn and Syd were now the parents of Samaria and Savion. Even though the twins were born prematurely and spent weeks in the hospital, they were now happy and healthy. At nine months old, they were crawling and all over the place. Syd and Camryn were now engaged and living better than they ever could have imagined. Camryn sometimes felt a little overwhelmed, being a new mother and trying to plan the perfect wedding, but she made it work. Syd had used some of his connections to land him a new job at Ensco on an oilfield platform as a galley hand supervisor.

Since he was gone for weeks at a time, Camryn was experiencing what it was like to be a single mother. Junior was also spending a lot of time with her and the kids, but she had no complaints because he was a big help. Ursula had finally grown up and was now back in school and co-parenting with Syd and Camryn for Fabian. She had finally put her big girl draws on and was acting more responsibly.

Phoenix and Jy were expecting a baby girl any day now. Phoenix couldn't wait to give birth, because she was just tired of being pregnant and swollen. Thankfully, Jy was adapting well to becoming a father. He loved Phoenix and he wanted nothing more than to keep her barefoot and pregnant. He couldn't wait for her to give birth, just so he could plant another seed inside of her. Phoenix was so in love with Jy and felt there was no greater feeling than having that love reciprocated. Jy was everything she needed and more and there was nothing that could ruin the bond they shared.

She had moved in with him permanently and he wouldn't have wanted it any other way. Phoenix and Camryn were still thick as thieves and she couldn't wait for her daughter to arrive, so that she could meet her little cousins, Samaria and Savion.

Phoenix never would have thought that things between Frederick and Brazailia would have escalated to the point that it did. They were the perfect example of why a man should never play with a woman's feelings. A woman scorned is also a dangerous woman. When the warrant was issued for Brazailia's arrest, following the discovery of Frederick's body, she left town immediately. Before she left, she entrusted Phoenix with her most precious gift; her and Frederick's son. She had been in hiding ever since.

At first, Phoenix was in shock that Brazailia had left her child with her, but she had grown to love the little boy and enjoyed having him around. She hated that things ended the way they did for Frederick, but she couldn't dwell on it and love Jy at the same time. So, she charged Frederick's death to the game and kept it moving.

Three weeks after Hennessy was booked on murder and arson charges of Club Lush, she confessed to those crimes, as well as burning Phoenix's house down. She felt with the way things were going, it might look good if she cooperated with the courts. She was hoping to get some leniency during sentencing. The judge sentenced her to twenty-five to life. While she was locked up, she had visited the infirmary on at least three separate occasions. She kept getting beat up by strippers who used to work at the club. They were pissed because they had plans to shake it fast once they were released. Hennessy served three hard months of her sentence before she was found hanging in her cell.

Drew's wife Jessica got her divorce and won her case against her ex-husband. She was allowed to keep the house, her SUV, and joint custody of the kids. Drew was ordered to pay fourteen hundred dollars a month in child support, which he despised, but had no choice. He finally decided to come out of the closet and recently started dating. He lost everything that he had worked so hard for, but he still had his peace of mind.

Tucker was still trying to find himself after all he had gone through. Denise cleaned out all their bank accounts, filed for divorce, and exposed Tucker to his entire family. His family disowned him, without a second thought. He no longer dealt with Drew and a part of him was glad. He felt that if it wasn't for Drew, none of this would have ever happened. He would still be married and living at home with his wife and kids. Drew ruined his life or so he said.

Rhianna, formerly known as Vicious, was now a full-time college student with a real nine to five job. She was on a positive path and refused to let anyone ruin it. She recently met a man and started dating him. He treats her like the queen her mother always told her she was. Hennessy's passing was one that hit a little too close to home. She could have gone down that same path if she hadn't decided to change her ways. Thank God she had such a strong support system. She thought a lot about Hennessy from time to time and wondered if there was anything she could have done to help her.

But the more she thought about it, the more she realized that Hennessy was responsible for herself. She could have turned everything around if she had just kept the faith.

The End!!

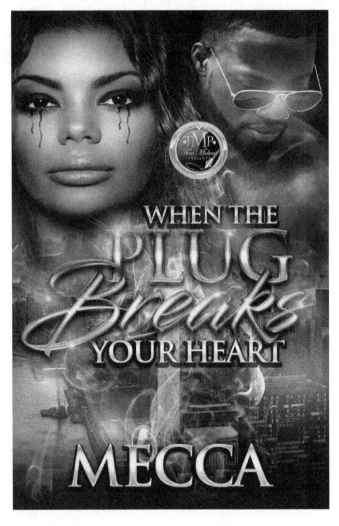

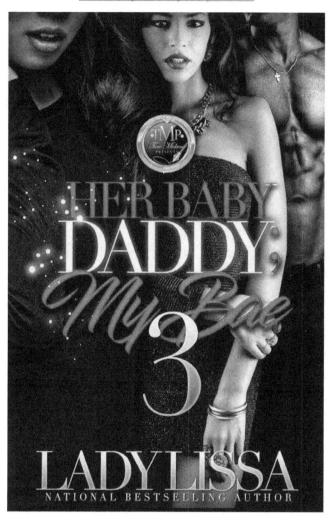

Are you looking for a
publishing home?

Tiece Mickens Presents, LLC
IS NOW ACCEPTING SUBMISSIONS
IN THE FOLLOWING *genres*

♛ African American Urban Fiction
♛ African American Romance
♛ Interracial Romance
♛ Women's Fiction
♛ Urban Erotica

Please Submit the first three chapters of your
manuscript via email to: submissions@tmpresents.com

We look forward to reading your work & possibly
bringing you aboard a winning team.

CPSIA information can be obtained
at www.ICGtesting.com
Printed in the USA
LVHW082017291218
602156LV00010B/106/P